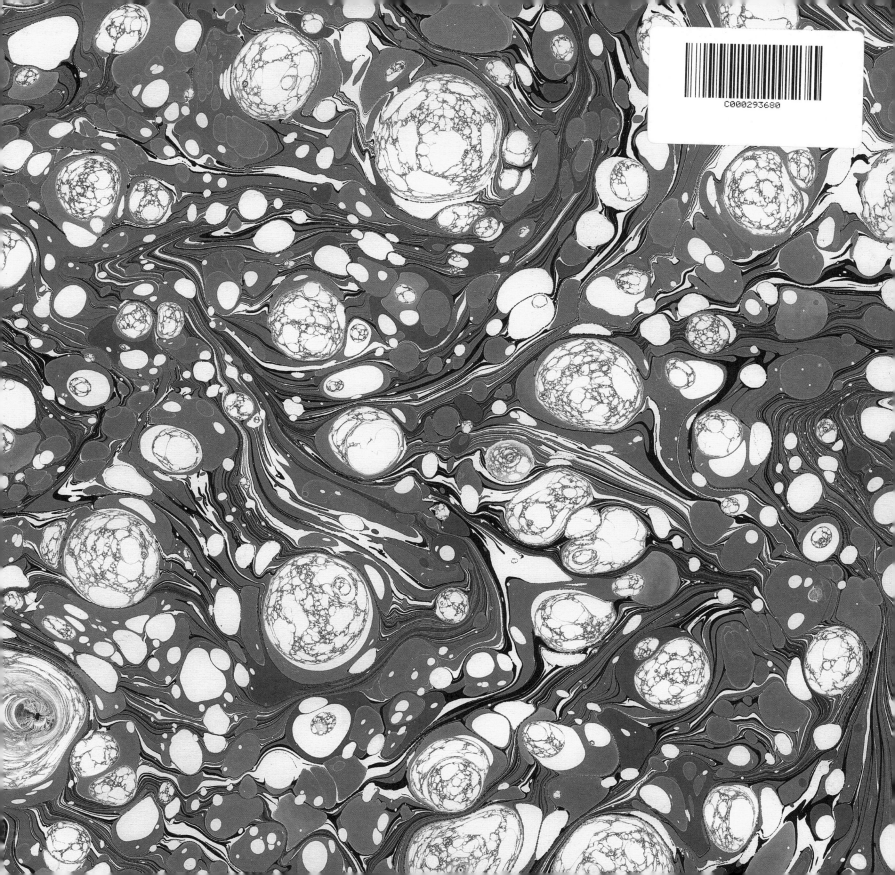

The Ankh-Morpork Archives

First published in Great Britain in 2019 by Gollancz an imprint of The Orion Publishing Group Ltd
Carmelite House, 50 Victoria Embankment London EC4Y 0DZ

An Hachette UK Company

1 4 7 3 2 0 5 3 5 2

A CIP catalogue record for this book is
available from the British Library.

ISBN (Hardback) 978 1 473205352

Layout and design by Vanessa Kidby and Alex Stott
Printed in Italy by Printer Trento S.r.l

www.orionbooks.co.uk
www.terrypratchett.com
www.discworld.com
www.paulkidby.com

THE Ankh-Morpork ARCHIVES

A Discworld Anthology
VOLUME 1

TERRY PRATCHETT
& STEPHEN BRIGGS

Illustrated by
PAUL KIDBY

CONTENTS

CONJURING UP
UNSEEN UNIVERSITY

We both enjoyed being able to play with and write down the stuff we knew hid behind UU's locked doors. Although neither Terry nor I had ever been to a 'real' university, I had the benefit of living in Oxford, and of having worked for a while for the Bodleian Library, one of the oldest libraries in Europe. We were also both fans of Tom Sharpe's 'Porterhouse Blue'. We had all we needed to build our own academic realm.

STEPHEN BRIGGS

It's hard to believe that I drew these pictures over twenty years ago. A lot of water has flowed (or mud has oozed, if we're talking about the River Ankh) under the bridge since then, but some things remain the same, such as my enduring enthusiasm for depicting the venerable faculty of Unseen University.

PAUL KIDBY

6

It's generally very quiet in the Unseen University library. There's perhaps the shuffling of feet as wizards wander between the shelves, the occasional hacking cough to disturb the academic silence, and every once in a while a dying scream as an unwary student fails to treat an old magical book with the caution it deserves.

TERRY PRATCHETT

UNSEEN

UNIVERSITY

Archchancellor's Address

I would like to take this opportunity to welcome this year's new students to Unseen University.

You are to be congratulated! For, by being born humans, male, and finding the talent to become wizards, you have thrown a treble six in the great dice game that is Life!

Well do I remember my first days at this College. Of course things were different then, rather than being the same as they are now. We no longer have characters like old 'Bogeyboy' Swallet, who took tutorials for more than three years after he was dead, or 'Metabolic' Stevenson, who once ate a live chicken by mistake. And I fondly recall 'Bendy' Twistler, who would hide behind the door of his study and actively try to kill any student who entered. We won't see his like again!! Of course, many students only saw his like once, and that very briefly. Naturally, wizardry in those days was more competitive than it is now and Prof. Twistler took the view that any youngster who couldn't fend off a simple axe blow had no business being here and would have come to a bad end in any case.

Times move on, of course (except in that little stretch of corridor next to the laundry, where for some reason it is still last year — you will be given some instructions about this), and I can assure you that any attempts on your life in your First and Second years will be accidental or at least only the result of a practical joke by fellow students, and if we couldn't laugh where would we be? I am always keen to see a sense of humour in my students although of course there are limits.

You will receive a thorough grounding in Magical Theory and Practice besides instruction in the sub-discipline of your choice, although I must tell you that I have decided to suspend Practical Necromancy after that unfortunate business with the shovel.

I realise that for many of you this will be your first time away from home, and I would like to think of us as one big family, with myself of course the father, and the Dean very well suited as a mother and the Bursar, for example, as that relative you have to go and visit every few weeks who smells rather peculiar. In loco parentis indeed. There is no doubt that we have a lot to learn from you young people, although I personally think I am already quite well informed on the subjects of being spotty, sulky and wearing hats on backwards. Nevertheless, we are here to listen to your little problems, perhaps rather too attentively in some cases, and I hope you will not hesitate to see me to discuss any difficulties you may have, although of course there is no excuse for lack of hygiene. I have always found that a refreshing cold bath and a brisk morning run solve most problems. My door is always open.

M. Ridcully

Mustrum Ridcully, D.Thau., D.M., D.S., D.Mn., D.G.,
D.D., D.C.L., D.M.Phil., D.M.S., D.C.M., D.W., B.El.L.
Archchancellor

UU TERMS

The University year is split into eight terms, each of which is approximately one week long in order to minimise the amount of time which the staff need to spend in the same room as the students.

Most students, however, continue to live in the University throughout much of the calendar year, undertaking their own research and generally absorbing magic from the fabric of the building and adding to its storehouse of knowledge.

The University terms follow the Great or true astronomical Disc year. We would like to give the precise dates, but they are announced at the discretion of the current Archchancellor, and sometimes many months or even years will go by without a term being officially opened. Look - frankly, 'terms' are regarded at UU as a tiresome and probably unnecessary interruption to the smooth running of the place. They spoil the routine and interfere with the proper workings of the bowels.

You know how to read. There is a library. You're here to learn, not be taught. If you want timetables, we suggest you try the stagecoach company.

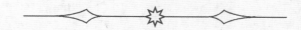

THE LIBRARY

We tell our students that there are some things that are sooner or later unavoidable, and these will probably include opening a book.

All students of Unseen University are entitled to use the Library, um, at the discretion of the Librarian. Unseen University's Library is accessible through the main building and various holes in the fabric of reality.

The UU Library is theoretically the largest in the universe or, indeed, any conceivable universe; it has a diameter of about one hundred yards but, as far as we can determine, an infinite radius. The presence of so much stored magic does to time and space what a hot iron does to a pound of butter, so that you may well encounter places where the floor is now the wall, the books have turned into small clay models of hedgehogs and you yourself appear to be a device for coring apples. Students will therefore find it convenient to stick to the routes marked with chalk and the occasional banana skin.

We must warn you that many students have cleverly worked out that since the Library does, somewhere, contain any book that will ever or could ever be written, their own doctoral thesis must be in there on some distant shelf. This is true.

Setting out to find it is, however, an extremely unwise move. We can assure you that, however long it takes, staying here and writing the damn thing is a lot easier in the end.

The main section of the Library, and the source of all the above difficulties, are the more than 90,000 volumes of magical books that are on and sometimes hovering slightly above its shelves.

Great care has to be taken to ensure that this magic causes no harm. On no account try to remove the copper strips nailed to the shelves. These are there for your protection! They earth the general magic leakage, and the penalty for taking them away, as one enterprising scrap merchant has already found, will be death if you are lucky. Large amounts of random magic can have such a chaotic effect on the human body.

You will notice that a great many of the books are in fact chained to the shelves. In most old libraries this would be to prevent them being stolen or damaged by people; in our Library, this is pretty much the other way about. If you move along the middle of the aisles and refrain from any overtly aggressive behaviour you will almost certainly survive.

Books that are borrowed must be returned no later than the last date shown. If you inadvertently lose or deface one, it is important to announce this to the Dean as soon as possible so that you may be smuggled out of college and helped to start a new life somewhere else. Our Librarian is very proud of his books, but somewhat intolerant of those who show them no respect or, indeed, even read them with too heavy a look, since one of his foibles is a belief that eyeball pressures can wear out the words.

On this subject students are advised to take the Librarian as they find him. Yes, he is an ape, but less vicious than most apes and many librarians. Gifts of nuts and soft fruit are acceptable, if proffered in the proper spirit. However tempting it may be to pull his leg, be advised that he can pull yours rather harder.

Users of the Library have certain responsibilities and therefore we print the:

DECLARATION TO BE READ ALOUD WHEN ASKED

'I, Speak Your Name, hereby undertake not to remove without permission from the Library, or to mark, deface, or injure in any way, any volume, document, or other object belonging to it, or use inappropriate force in fighting back any such volumes as may from time to time attack me; not to bring into the Library or kindle therein any fire or flame be it magical or otherwise, and not to smoke or expectorate or explode or levitate above 2' in the Library; to refrain, to the best of my abilities, from spontaneously combusting in the Library; and I promise to obey all rules of the Library and any which may, from time to time, be added by the Librarian, whose judgement on all matters relating to the operation of the Library is final and if necessary terminal. I further promise to read and inwardly digest any documents that are drawn to my attention attesting to the difference between those creatures commonly referred to as "monkeys" and the higher apes, accepting further that being allowed to do so is a concession on the part of the Librarian, that holding my head two inches from the page facilitates reading and that repeatedly banging it on the table is a valuable aid to memory.'

18

ATTENDING LECTURES

Actually, this is not as bad as it sounds. The Faculty were all students themselves and understand the rules.

In this matter they are easily understood but hard to explain. In short, however, failure to attend lectures is considered acceptable provided that what you are doing is formally failing to attend lectures, in a deliberate, nay, thoughtful way.

To rephrase it for philosophy students: Does Sergeant Detritus of the City Watch fail to attend lectures? Clearly not. He merely does not go to them. Lectures do not figure in his world view. *Failing to attend lectures*, however, is a very deliberate activity, in which the student, wherever he is, *defines himself as not being somewhere else.* (See *Psychological Places*, by E. R. Clamp, D.Thau., Egregious Professor of Cruel and Unusual Geography, UU.) The distinction here is between *dynamic* and merely passive and unthinking non-attendance. If stopped in the streets by a member of staff, a student who can say in a firm, clear voice, 'Sir I am *currently not attending* Professor Didymus' lecture on Thaumic Equivalency' (or whatever other event is currently being not attended), will be allowed to go on his way. It is important that new students get a grip on this idea, since merely bunking off is severely punished.

HAT SIZES

Hats come in all sizes. The trick is to keep trying different ones on until you find one that fits you. The idea is to stick your head in the hole.

CLOTHES SIZES

See 'Hat Sizes', although there are more holes.

UNSEEN UNIVERSITY
JCR, Peach Pie Street, Ankh-Morpork

Dear Fresher,

Hey, wow, congratulations on gaining your place at Unseen University and welcome to Ankh-Morpork! Those sad old dudes on the University faculty have allowed us free-thinking, with-it, radical, bodacious guys to take over a whole page of this Official Diary in order to welcome you to Unseen University as it really is!

??

Your time at Unseen University should be the highest point in your life so far. You now have access to some of the most crucial clubs and hottest nightlife that this most cosmopolitan of cities can offer! Hey, even a cool dude like me can remember how inadequate, sad and utterly, utterly homesick you're bound to feel!

We hold a big bash in the JCR (that's the Junior Common Room, for you newbies) on Day Five of 0th week to welcome you all, give you a chance to see what clubs and societies the University has to offer and, well, more to the point, to get completely ratted!

If there's anything at all that you need to know about the University or about the great city of Ankh-Morpork, please don't hesitate to pop in and see me!

I look forward to meeting you all!!

Yours in wizardry,

Adrian

Adrian Turnipseed

JCR President

22

Dear Mr. Turnipseed,

I have read your copy. I am not at all certain what is radical and free-thinking about sitting up all night in the High Energy Magic building trying to teach Hex to play 'Barbarian Invaders' and living on pizza; what precisely is 'it' that you are 'with'?; I have looked in vain for a meaning for 'bodacious'; and I object to the suggestion that the Faculty are 'sad' and, moreover, have no concept of modern colloquial usage. Far from being unhappy, as you suggest, we are frequently rather gay.

M.R.

Dear Mr. Turnipseed,

I do not object to this paragraph insofar as I understand any of it. Clearly if you are indeed cool, going somewhere hot would seem to be a good idea.

M.R.

Dear Mr. Turnipseed,

Perhaps you could drop into my office shortly to explain this paragraph. M.R.

SOCIETIES & CLUBS

OFFLER'S LEAGUE OF TEMPERANCE

c/o 57, *Lobbin Clout*

To be frank, not many student wizards have joined this one over the years. In fact it only has one member, who is frequently off with injuries owing to his attempts to play ping-pong against himself. The League holds whist drives and cheese & squash evenings. It also used to host the Sto Plains Tiddly-Wink Finals, which are held every year in Sektober, although these have been banned after the damage caused when Troll Rules' winking was introduced.

ANKH-MORPORK HISTORICAL RE-CREATION SOCIETY

Midden Street

The Society exists for the research into and re-creation of the great battles of the Ankh-Morpork Civil War and earlier times, although bystanders believe that the research aspect consists largely of seeing how much beer can be drunk while still allowing a man to hold his pike. Volunteers to be sabre-fodder are always welcome. The soft jobs on horseback are not for the likes of you.

FRIENDLY FLAMETHROWERS' LEAGUE

12, *Pons Bridge*

One of the city's many clubs and societies for those who keep or breed swamp dragons. The League organises charitable events to raise funds to protect swamp dragons and also help members settle the enormous legal and rebuilding costs that come from keeping them. Warning: students found keeping a dragon in their rooms will be fined and, if enough of their body parts can be found in the wreckage, expelled from college.

ANKH-MORPORK FINE ART APPRECIATION SOCIETY

Shamlegger Street

A society devoted to the finer points of the female form. The Society frequently holds artistic evenings where members can paint live models, and no one enquires too deeply as to whether they actually have any paint on their brushes.

MORPORK FOLK DANCE & SONG CLUB

c/o The Bunch of Grapes, Easy Street

If you like songs about how good it was when everyone used to eat mud, and you call all kinds of beer 'ale' and can make a half-pint last all evening, this is the place for you. Things have been improved recently by a new Club rule banning all songs beginning 'As I was a-walking' or 'Come all ye bold seafaring lads'. Meetings are now a lot shorter. Before you buy a half-pint of beer you have to sing a song about how good the old one was.

25

PLACES TO GO, THINGS TO SEE

THE OPERA HOUSE
Pseudolpolis Yard

Tours backstage can be arranged with the Stage Manager, Mr Arno. Since the appointment of Mr Plinge as Musical Director, the Opera House has become a much safer place to visit. However, the current owner of the House is well aware of the value of tradition, and since the recent notoriety he has arranged special performances twice daily where singers are terrorised and young ladies may be abducted by appointment. These are held at noon and 3 p.m. precisely.

THE BUREAU OF MEASURES
The Barbican, Street of Small Gods

This was established by Olaf Quimby, past Patrician of Ankh-Morpork, and is keenly supported by the current Patrician. The Bureau still sets the standards for weights, measures and time, both within the city and beyond, and has built up strong links with the University.

Its original offices still house the standard examples of such items as the official Two Short Planks (as in 'thick as') and the stone used in the original moss-gathering trials. Entry is at the discretion of the Curator. Of course, the place is not only a museum. Research goes on all the time, and the student in search of a bit of spare cash can often find temporary employment in one of the programmes. Recent tests have proved that, with care, a quite passable silk purse can be made out of a sow's ear, and the relevant proverb has now been banned in the city on pain of an AM$100 fine.

On-going, long-term experiments are being undertaken on 'Soft words butter no parsnips', and researchers with a variety of voices are being sought to shout, rant and cajole an experimental rig consisting of a) some butter and b) some parsnips. The proverb is now being tentatively replaced by 'Only a knife butters some parsnips'. However, research is showing up some interesting results with turnips. A much more extensive experiment, for which volunteers are always being sought, is in the Watched Pot laboratory, and there is some exciting evidence that may overturn current theories about the boiling point of water. The 'Fool and his Money are Soon Parted' test rig has now been dismantled following the unfortunate accident.

27

THE POST OFFICE
Upper Broad Way

One of the city's more picturesque public buildings, the Post Office traditionally handled the massive volume of letters and packets which passed between the city and the four corners of the Disc. Unfortunately, what with one thing and another, a few wars, the city's general bankruptcy, the fact that no one was getting paid and so on, this enviable system collapsed long ago and people now find it easier to give any mail to a passing dwarf.

Provided it does not look edible or appear to contain money, this is in fact quite a sensible system. There are dwarfish colonies in all major cities on the Sto Plains, the dwarf traffic between them is immense, and for a small fee the dwarfs will get your mail to its destination. For a rather larger fee, they won't open it and read the more interesting paragraphs to their friends on the way.

Though reliable, this arrangement is on the slow side, and the best time to post your Hogswatch cards is a few weeks before the previous Hogswatch.

In the meantime the huge Post Office building languishes unoccupied except for ravens, gargoyles, rats, a few people of the crusty-clothed persuasion and, of course, the Post Master, a hereditary Royal appointment which has never been extinguished. Since the salary has never been increased for centuries either, and is two dollars a year, the current incumbent is keen to show visitors around in exchange for food or items of warm clothing.

Do not miss – and how could you – the estimated five hundred tons of ancient undelivered mail that accumulated in the Post Office during its final disastrous days. Students of history are often to be found on the lower slopes, where every shovelful yields a new delight.

28

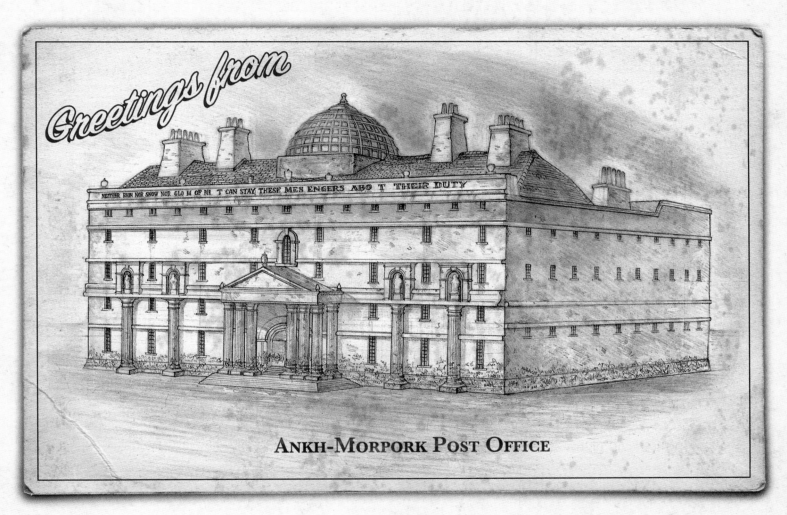

ANKH-MORPORK POST OFFICE

29

CEMETERY OF THE TEMPLE OF SMALL GODS
Street of Cunning Artificers

Many of the city's better-known historical figures are buried here. A large denomination coin will usually gain you access to the grave of Lady Alice Venturi, with its decoration of 'educational' Al-Ybian frescoes (provided your party includes no unmarried women under the age of 30). Other notable graves include those of Weaven Trump, inventor of the potato. A few of Ankh-Morpork's undead community maintain mausoleums there, and are only too happy to show unwary visitors around by appointment.

THE TANTY
Lag Lane

Although the torture chambers and oubliettes are now no longer used under Lord Vetinari's enlightened government of the city (some would say 'endarkened', but not us), they are retained to delight the parties of schoolchildren who regularly visit in order to be shown by their teachers what will become of them if they don't try to be teachers when they grow up. A modest charge is made for use of the Rack.

JIMKIN BEARHUGGER'S DISTILLERY
Wet Alley

Mr Bearhugger's produce is known and remembered throughout the Disc. He and his staff are always keen to welcome visitors who, for a mere dollar, will be given a guided tour of the distillery which includes a free tot of Jimkin Bearhugger's Old Selected Dragon's Blood Whiskey ('Every bottle matured for up to seven minutes'). The impecunious student may pick up occasional work here taking visitors back to their homes (please bring your own wheelbarrow).

THE RUINS
The Tump

These are believed to be the ruins of the original Royal Palace, although records were destroyed long ago. They are picturesque and afford a fine view of the city, if that is your idea of fun. Many people make the circuitous journey and stay at the top long enough to say 'Oh' and 'Do you think we can get down to the shops before they close?' Not open to coach parties of more than six people, nor to those mounted on horses or oxen.

THE MORPORK SUNSHINE SANCTUARY FOR SICK DRAGONS

Morphic Street

This charitable institution is always happy to see visitors with money or, failing that, their own dunging fork and protective clothing.

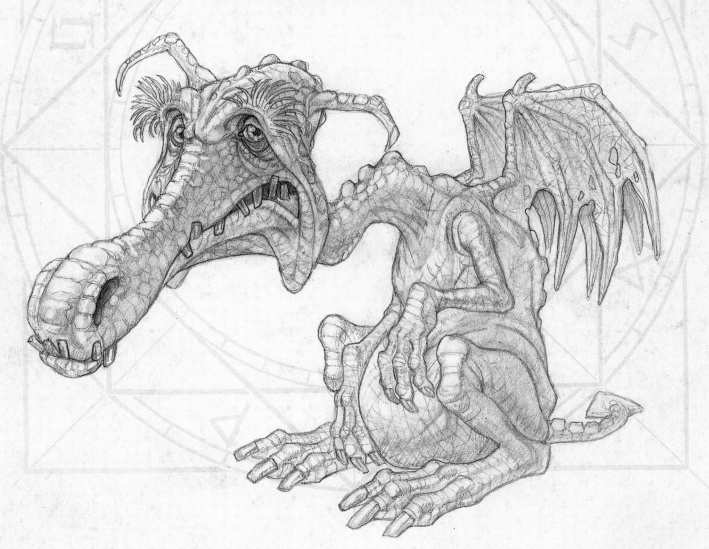

31

DWARF BREAD MUSEUM
Whirligig Alley

This is open throughout the normal dwarfish working day (i.e. 24 hours) and contains the finest display of historic dwarf bread and battle bread outside the Ramtops. It has recently been refurbished following the tragic death of the previous owner and is being run on a temporary basis by the Campaign for Equal Heights, who have tried to get away from the dusty old image and now run evening classes in offesive dough kneading and unarmed crumpet. Many of the new exhibits are interactive – that is to say, the bread just sits there and people can look at it and read the labels to one another very slowly – and on most fine afternoons there are outdoor displays of bread hurling. Entry is 2p.

BARS

Ankh-Morpork is blessed with a vast number of watering holes (that is to say, holes where the beer is watered) of varying standards, and newcomers to the city will have no problem finding somewhere to buy a drink. Some of the city's more . . . well, let's call them *picturesque* inns are worth a special mention, though.

THE MENDED DRUM
Filigree Street (end of Short Street)

This is, by general agreement, the city's premier ale-house. There has been an inn on this site since the city was founded. Originally it was known as the Broken Drum ('You Can't Beat It') but was renamed after its last rebuilding, following a city fire believed to have been started in its cellars. Unfortunately, notoriety seems to have gone to its head, and it is suspected that some of the fights and most of the more gruesome murders are now merely staged for visitors, leading to its boycott by the Campaign for Real Mayhem. Good peanuts, though, and the Barbarian Invaders machine gives you an extra go every time ever since the Librarian blew beer into the slot.

THE BUCKET
Gleam Street

This pub is one frequented by the Ankh-Morpork City Watch. This might make it one of the city's safer pubs, but the downside is that you end up drinking with some of the city's least savoury inhabitants (the Watch). Good for gossip.

BUNCH OF GRAPES
Easy Street

One of those pubs where they look at you carefully when you enter in case it'd be easier to kill you than go to all the trouble of serving you, but worth it for the genuine scumble cider, brought all the way from the Ramtops. Only drunk by those with more teeth than brain cells, but this is not important since if you drink enough of it you won't have any of either.

CRIMSON LEECH
Easy Street

Good sawdust, watery beer. The owner's wife does a good Knuckle Sandwich.

TROLL'S HEAD
The Shades

To be frank, this one is best avoided unless you seek a quick but painful death. True, you'll get beaten and stabbed in The Mended Drum as well, but at least there they'll have a bit of a laugh about it.

KING'S HEAD
Moon Pond Lane

Good ale. Passable bar snacks. Shame about the publican's dog. Don't wear expensive trousers.

BIERS
(formerly the Crown and Dagger)
Elm Street

This is where you may end up drinking if you failed to heed our advice about the Troll's Head. It is an *undead* bar. If you really must enter, don't drink anything that isn't in a clear glass, avoid the bar munchies and never, ever eat one of the barman Igor's 'pickled eggs'. But be warned: it really is best avoided. You may think you look good in black clothes and heavy eyeliner, but in Biers they'll think you'd look good on toast.

37

STAB IN THE BACK
corner of Salis Street and Pseudopolis Yard

This pub is close to the Opera House and is therefore conveniently situated for drinkies before or after or, preferably, *during* productions. Overpriced. During the intervals, the casual customer is likely to be crushed by the rush of opera musicians desperate to down eight or nine pints in the fifteen minutes before the curtain next goes up. However, tagging along after them can often mean that you get a really good seat for nothing, if looking up divas' dresses is your idea of fun. You may, however, be expected to play some sort of instrument, but since the audience is used to a certain spontaneity in the tunes after the interval, lack of any skill will not be a major problem.

EATERIES

It is difficult to decide which of Ankh-Morpork's many ethnic, fast food and other eateries to single out for a mention, so we have relied on including those who've paid us a small wedge.

HARGA'S HOUSE OF RIBS

The Shades. Follow your nose.

Harga serves any sort of food you can name, provided you don't have much imagination and it can be cooked in gallons of beef dripping (ask about their deep-fried custard). Harga's All-You-Can-Gobble-For-A-Dollar menu is famous wherever huge appetites gather, although he has banned students because apparently they can gobble far too much. You don't want to know about the salad bar.

LAUGHING FALAFEL
(Klatchian Take-Away & All-Nite Grocery)

Sniggs Alley (off Welcome Soap)

The Laughing Falafel caters well for those persons whose tastes tend towards the non-meat end of the dietary spectrum - that is to say, the *deliberate* non-meat end, since what turns up in some pies and sausages in Ankh-Morpork often does not qualify (remember . . . just because it's been inside an animal doesn't make it meat).

GROANING PLATTER

corner of Frost Alley and Flood Walk

Good salad bar, but the 'all you can get in the bowl for 10 pence' facility has been withdrawn since a student from the Faculty of Thaumic Engineering perfected his Tiny Salad Bar Bowl-of-Holding, capable of taking three tons of assorted lettuce and tomato.

RON'S PIZZA HOVEL

Clarty Street

41

Just about anything you can think of to eat that can be fitted on to a pizza. We really mean that. Try the Herring and Banana Deep Pan Surprise. Sometimes the surprise takes as long as fifteen minutes.

FAT SALLY'S

Squeezebelly Alley, Isle of Gods

Famous for its take-away sandwiches and rolls and for its selection of the Disc's coffees. High-quality doughnuts.

CURRY GARDENS

corner of God Street and Blood Alley

The Curry Gardens serve some of the best if least authentic Klatchian food in Ankh-Morpork. Death is said to eat there but does not, in a professional sense, get involved in take-away.

43

44

GIMLET'S HOLE FOOD DELICATESSEN

Cable Street

Probably best known for its dwarfish rat cuisine, although it is now 'generic ethnic' and caters for most human and non-human visitors, leading to many 'cross-over' dishes of greater or lesser edibility. Trolls may find the chalk-and-chicken tikka palatable, but humans should steer clear of the fossilised ammonite cocktail.

ENTERTAINMENTS

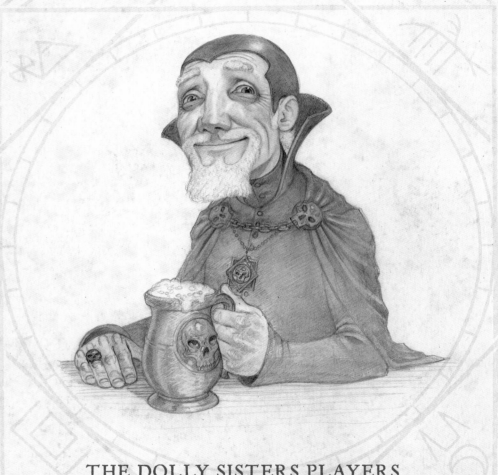

THE DOLLY SISTERS PLAYERS

Dolly Sisters

An amateur dramatics society, a leading light of which is Doctor Hix, Professor in Post-Mortem Communication. Free tickets are often available (check your pockets) as part of Dr Hix's efforts to spread darkness and despondency throughout the world by means of amateur dramatics.

THE BEAR PIT
Lower Broad Way

This theatre started with live animal shows, but now concentrates on the sort of plays that tread a fine line between real theatre and the sort of performances that, performed on the streets, would quickly earn the players an extended stay in the Patrician's scorpion pit. Only worth a visit if your parents are avant-garde.

THE ANKH-MORPORK EXPERIENCE
Chrononhotonthologos Street

Experience the sights, sounds and smells of the Disc's greatest city without any of the dangers that go with actually walking in its streets. Visitors are conveyed on quaint replica tumbrils through an accurate representation of the city of Ankh-Morpork whilst a live commentary from a gnome sitting on your shoulder tells you all about the city's history, places to avoid, etc. The best way for out-of-townies to safely see the city.

47

THE DYSK
off Lower Broad Way

The Dysk was built by Mr O. Vitoller. Most of the plays are written by the renowned dwarf playwright, Hwel. Whilst the plays are often unremarkable, most of them star Mr Vitoller's son, Tomjon, who is an actor of such astounding ability that the quality of the play is often unimportant. A must for your parents.

LORD WYNKIN'S MEN
Lower Broad Way

A well-intentioned group who specialise in comedies of mistaken identity, featuring men who lose their trousers and ladies who spend much of the plays in their foundation garments. Much frequented by student wizards and students from the city's various Guilds.

SWAMP DRAGONS

STAGES OF THEIR DEVELOPMENT

Many students choose a swamp dragon as a pet (usually having been talked into it during a visit to the Sunshine Sanctuary). It is important to know the stages of your pet's development and some of the terminology you'll need to recognise when talking to other owners:

HEN . . . . *A female swamp dragon*

PEWMET . . . . *A male swamp dragon under the age of eight months*

COCK . . . . *A male swamp dragon between the age of eight and fourteen months*

SNOOD . . . . *A male swamp dragon between the age of fourteen months and two years*

COBB . . . . *A male swamp dragon over two years old and still living*

CRATER . . . . *A male swamp dragon after death*

WHITTLE . . . . *A runt, or bad purchase*

SLUMP . . . . *A group of swamp dragons numbering more than two animals*

EMBARRASSMENT . . . . *A group of swamp dragons between one and two in number*

DEBRIS . . . . *Less than one whole swamp dragon*

CURRENCY CONVERSION CHART

The currency in Ankh-Morpork is the Dollar, which consists of 100 pence. The following gives a rough conversion for the Disc's other major currencies:

Agatean Rhinu...................... *Well, forget it. One gold Rhinu could probably buy several streets in Ankh-Morpork, but the Agateans haven't worked this out, and since lead seems to be very rare in their country some suitable rate of exchange may yet be arrived at*

Borogravian Zloty .... *eight to the AM$*

Brindisian Lire..................... *one thousand and six to the AM$*

Djelibeybian Talent.................. *two thousand, one hundred and thirty-one to the AM$*

Ephebian Derechmi.................. *eight and three quarters to the AM$*

Genuan Dollar .... *one and a half to the AM$*

Hershebian Dong.................... *four hundred to the AM$*

Howondaland Wichit Bead .... *eight hundred and sixty to the AM$*

Istanzian Dinar..................... *forty-seven to the AM$*

Klatchistani Wol .... *about three to the AM$*

Lancre Penny .... *one hundred to the AM$*

Llamedosian Cumri.................. *twenty-six to the AM$*

Omnian Obol .... *three AM$ to each Obol*

Überwaldian Kram .... *four to the AM$*

Zchloty Iotum .... *seventeen thousand five hundred to each AM$*

LORD VETINARI'S WORDS OF WISDOM

Someone must be punished for every crime. If it is the perpetrator, this is a happy bonus.

Taxation is the art of getting the most milk for the least moo.

What people really want is that tomorrow should be no worse than today.

It is quite amazing what men will do if forbidden to do it with sufficient emphasis.

Learn The Words.

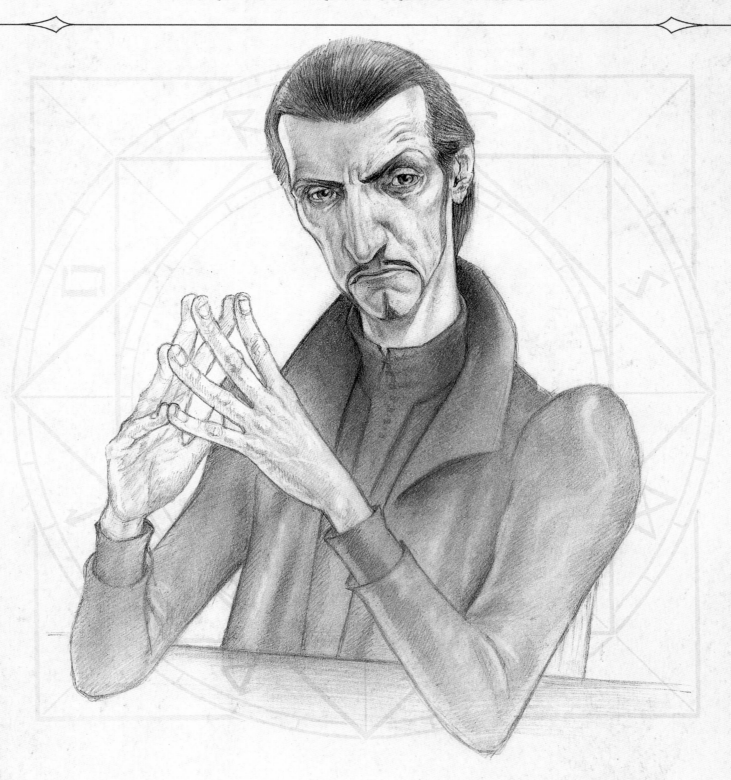

53

UNSEEN UNIVERSITY FACULTY & STAFF

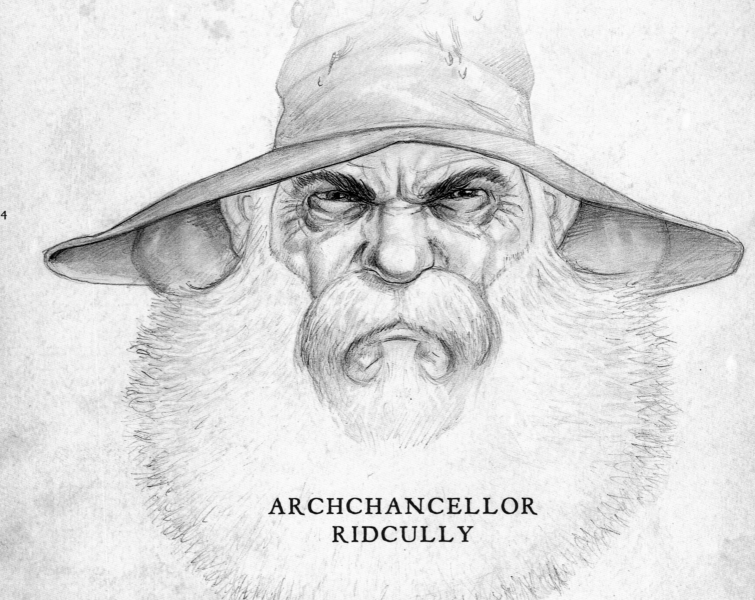

ARCHCHANCELLOR
RIDCULLY

THE BURSAR

THE DEAN

RECENT RUNES

SENIOR WRANGLER

THE LIBRARIAN

PONDER STIBBONS

DOCTOR HIX

CHAIR OF INDEFINITE STUDIES

57

Wizards were like weather vanes, or the canaries that miners used to detect pockets of gas. They were by their nature tuned to an occult frequency. If there was anything strange happening, it tended to happen to wizards first.

Soul Music

58

It was amazing how fast you could run with a couple of bledlows behind you – through the foggy night-time streets.

Unseen Academicals

59

Modo's compost heaps heaved and fermented and glowed faintly in the dark,
perhaps because of the mysterious and possibly illegal ingredients Modo fed them.

Reaper Man

To answer such questions Hex had been built, although Ponder Stibbons was a bit uneasy about the word 'built' in this context. He and a few keen students had put it together, certainly, but...well... sometimes he thought bits of it, strange though this sounded, just turned up.

Interesting Times

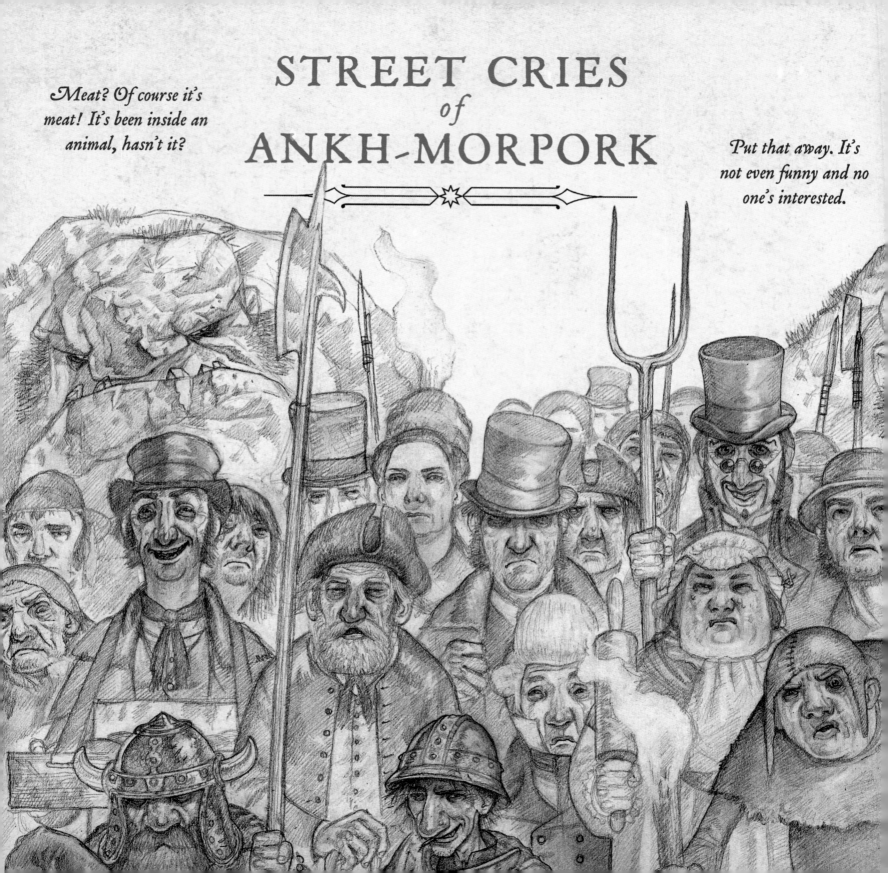

STREET CRIES
of
ANKH-MORPORK

Meat? Of course it's meat! It's been inside an animal, hasn't it?

Put that away. It's not even funny and no one's interested.

Wizards did not have balls. There was a popular song about it. But they did hold their annual Excuse Me, or free-for-all dance, which was one of the highlights of the Ankh-Morpork social calendar. The Librarian in particular always looked forward to it, and used an amazing amount of hair cream.

Soul Music

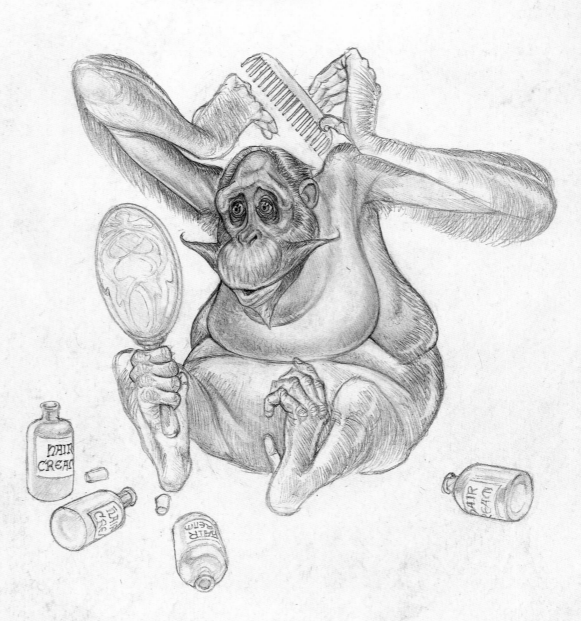

THE CUT AND THRUST OF
THE ASSASSINS' GUILD

It was fun for Terry, and a delight for me, to build some more detailed reality supporting the facades of the institutions which form Ankh-Morpork. We both loved Anthony Buckeridge's 'Jennings and Darbishire' books (and I included a couple of tiny homages). The Assassins' Guild offers the best all-round education on Discworld. I was therefore very grateful to Eton College, who allowed me time in their library to access and research their records of traditions and ceremonies.

STEPHEN BRIGGS

It was fun to delve deep into the Assassins' Guild - and come out alive! This book gave me the opportunity to draw a slew of assassins and the tools of their bloody trade. Highlights were designing an exploding bustle (Terry's favourite) and pondering the dietary habits of the Sumtri fire newt.

PAUL KIDBY

He ... had also heard that only one student in fifteen actually became an assassin. He wasn't entirely certain what happened to the other fourteen, but he was pretty sure that if you were a poor student in a school for assassins they did a bit more than throw the chalk at you, and that the school dinners had an extra dimension of uncertainty.

TERRY PRATCHETT

NIL MORTE, SINE LVCRO

ASSASSINS'

GUILD

70

Head Master's Address

I would like to take this opportunity to welcome to the Guild of Assassins (Conlegium Sicariorum) those boys, and especially those girls, who have joined the Guild this Term.

'CS', as you will hear the Guild referred to by Masters and pupils, has a long and, on occasion, proud history. Our Old Boys have gone on to make their mark in politics, religion, and all branches of government. Admittedly, in many cases, those marks have been difficult to see with the naked eye, mainly because we pride ourselves on not being unnecessarily messy.

Many Old Sicarians now hold offices of great power and authority on the Disc: King Pteppicymon XXXXX of Djelibeybi and our own, much loved, Lord Vetinari (currently the Provost of the Conlegium), to name but two.

Here at the Guild we pride ourselves on educating the whole person (experiments in educating small parts of them having failed in the past) on all aspects of social life and, of course, death. As well as the subjects of direct relevance to the Guild's foundation, we also provide a thorough grounding, which is second to none, in subjects as diverse as Languages, Drawing, Quartering — just my little joke — Geography, Dance & Drama, Alchemy, Embroidery, Advanced Weaponry, History, Brewing and all manner of out-door sports. I myself take sixth-formers for advanced classes in poisoning, and I can assure you that my wife's Thursday afternoon teas, which they are expected to attend, are an education in themselves.

An Old Sicarian can hold up his or her head — or in some cases on unusual assignments someone else's head — in polite society, secure in the knowledge that he (or she) has been trained to deal with any situation that may arise, particularly if it involves edged weapons.

And thereby hangs a great misunderstanding. People seem to believe that the Assassins' Guild school trains its pupils to kill people. I cannot imagine how they got that idea. Of course, many alumni do go on to join that most select branch of the diplomatic profession, but increasing numbers of you are, I know, joining as Oppidans, quite correctly seeking to benefit from our superb education without intending eventual 'field' membership of the Guild. In this we are moving with the times.

Some of you, I dare to hope, will find our curriculum bringing out from within you certain . . . talents which a life in the Guild will allow you to develop to the full. But all of you, as you make your way in the world and possibly attract the envy of others who may therefore employ the Guild against you, may well have cause to bless the day that you paid attention in the classes on Defence Techniques.

Nevertheless, the Assassin is no murderer. A trained Assassin has honour, flair, panache, a certain je ne sais quoi. Above all, an Assassin has Rules. No mere muggers in dark alleyways we. Ahem, . . . let me rephrase that . . . we are not mere muggers in dark alleyways, or exponents of the long-range crossbow. We do not shoot people down in the street. We inhume with style, elegance and care. The client – and we take the view that it is the recipient of the service who should be termed 'the client' – will always be given a chance, if they are alert or provident or observant enough, to escape, evade or even defeat the Assassin. Anything else is mere butchery. Worse than that, anything else is bad manners.

And I may say that should you in later life find your path is crossed by a member of the Guild, you will have the warm, if brief, satisfaction of knowing that you have been inhumed by a fellow Sicarian who has learned tact, skill and the arts of painlessness.

I would like to take this opportunity to welcome a few newcomers. Firstly, I'm sure that many of you have already heard of Miss Alice Band, who comes to us fresh from her recent expedition to the lost Spider Temple of Fafaree, where she succeeded not only in getting all three parts of the Golden Sword of the Spider God, but also rendered no fewer than five endangered species completely extinct! There is a lesson there for all of us!

A welcome too to our new sports master, Mr Ifor Bradlofrudd, from Llamedos, who will be taking over responsibility for Sport and Hand-to-Hand Combat and will, I understand, be introducing a tribal game which neatly combines both.

Let me also extend the hand of friendship to the scholarship boys. The Guild has always regretted that accidents of birth or wealth close the door on a Guild career to many young people, and so there are a number of Guild and individual scholarships every year. Four new boys, survivors of the rather boisterous competitive entrance examination, will be joining up this year in Welcome Soap House and will be allowed to mix with the fee-paying pupils in carefully controlled circumstances.

We also welcome Jasper 'James' Chrysoprase, nephew of Mr Chrysoprase the well-respected businesstroll, who comes from excellent strata. I am sure he will do famously.

But, of course, the most exciting news this year is that we are opening our doors to the fairer, I dare not say weaker sex, ahaha, for the first time. The first light of the Century of the Anchovy will find us a fully co-educational establishment (within reasonable limits, of course). No longer will the sisters of our pupils have to languish at home, forced to practise their skills with girlish inexpertise on the domestic staff, hah hah. Of course, we know now that some were not content to remain so and enrolled anyway, relying on a short haircut and a forged note from their parents about doing sport. Mme les Deux-Épées herself (now the House Tutor of the new all-girl BlackWidow House, formerly Tarantula House) famously became Captain of Fencing here without causing comment beyond the fact that 'he' was rather shy in the showers.

I am quite sure that before too long the girls of BlackWidow and the proposed Mantis House will be showing us all that the female of the species is deadlier than the male and, of course, rather more attractive.

In conclusion, I would like to assure you that the staff of CS are here to help you. If you are in distress please speak to your Prefects who will, if necessary, refer you to your Tutor, to the Scullion or to me. My door is always open. Well, my window is always open – doors are too easy for students at Old Sicarius, haha.

Remember our watchword – It is a Noble Thing to Lay Down Someone Else's Life for Your Country. And, of course, to get a receipt.

Collegium Sicariorum

Memorandum

To All Staff
From the Head Master

I must tell you all that, following the experiment last term, the Guild Council has voted to accept young ladies on the roll this year. I am aware that a number of you have strong feelings on this issue, but there you are. We must be seen to move with the times.

We are also taking on our first troll. Again, I am aware of the arguments. However, the Chrysoprase family is paying for the new Alchemy laboratory and I have met the young troll in question. He has an exuberant tendency to violence that only needs harnessing to practical purposes for him to become a valuable member of the Guild.

Incidentally, I have noticed a growing tendency for boys to go around the City without their hands in their pockets, and in some cases even to progress with a firm, upright step. Assassins — even in training — do not march. They move with a languid, even louche step, and tend to lean against things and yawn in a knowing way. Any boy found sitting up straight is to be sent to my study immediately. To be a pupil here is to be a lord of creation. People expect an Assassin to have a certain style, after all. Without style, we are rather expensive thugs.

I am sure you will all be pleased to learn that no less than AM$1,100 was raised for a memorial plaque to Mr Stanley 'Touché' Danpipe (Fencing) whose clean death at the end of last term at the hands of P. Phelps, Lower Fifth, was a lesson to us all in both style and duty. It will be engraved with his last words, which were *Very good, boy. A marked improvement since last year. Aaargh.*

74

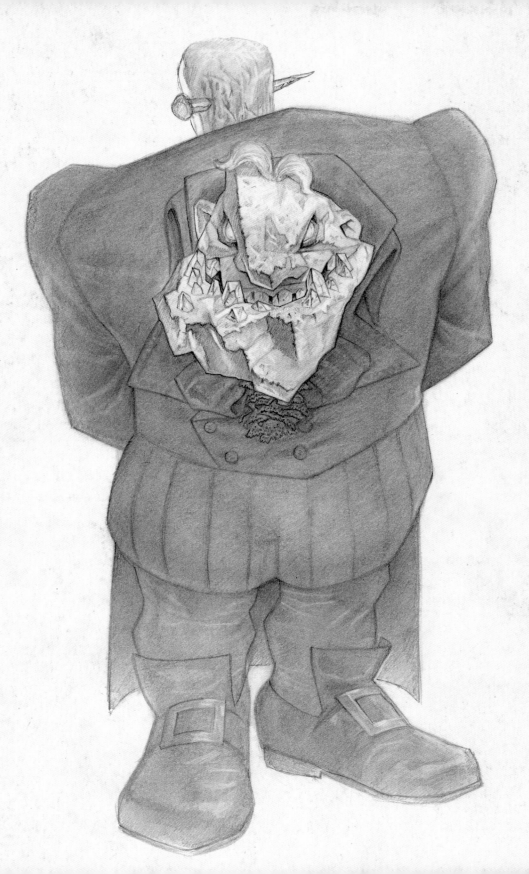

FINDING YOUR WAY AROUND

On arrival at the Guild, you will be greeted by your House Master, who will appoint an older boy to act as your guide for your first few days at CS. The following are brief descriptions of the main areas of the Guild that you'll need to be familiar with in your early days.

A BRIEF STROLL AROUND THE MAIN QUAD

Do not neglect the Porter's Lodge, wherein may be found Stippler the porter. His father was porter here, as was *his* father. He has seen it all, and the few bits he hasn't seen he can guess at. Do not attempt to play japes on him. He will remember your face, and you will find your time here clouded by all the many ways a school porter can make a boy's life a subtle misery. Tip him a shilling and the world will be a happier place.

Your path will then lead out into the quadrangle, dominated by its statue of Ellis William Netley, the student who, when playing the Wall Game, first picked up the ball and hurled it with such force that he knocked an opposing player off a second-storey window ledge. He was beaten senseless for this, but his action changed the Game from the rather insipid ball game that it was to the thrilling and bloody spectacle it is today.

To one side of the quad you can still see the new masonry of the repair to the museum wall after the unfortunate events concerning the removal from office of the previous Master, Dr Cruces. You will learn more about this early in your stay here. let us just say for now that he was tempted to disobey one of the major rules of the Guild.

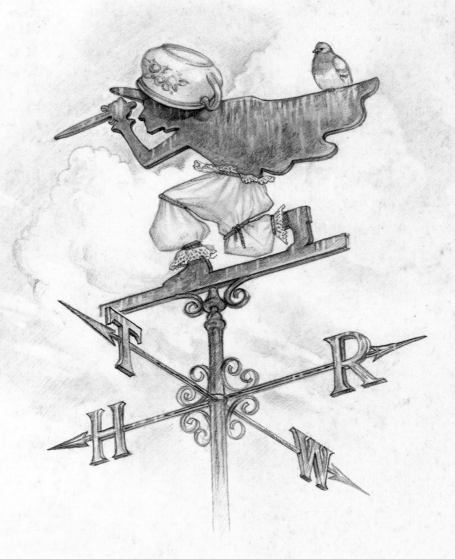

Looking up, you can see the bell tower, topped by the Guild's famous cloaked man weathervane (known as 'Wiggy Charlie'), which has oft been decked with porcelain chamberpots and female undergarments by waggish students on **Wag Days**.

Returning to the cloister, we turn and walk along, past the oil paintings and busts of famous inhumees. The first bust, of a former Crown Prince of Brindisi, is now almost unrecognisable as generations of student Assassins have patted his regal nose for luck. His plaque records that he 'Departed this vale of tears on 3 Grune, Year of the Sideways Leech, with the assistance of the Hon. K. W. Dobson (Viper House)'.

We now turn to the Combination Corridor, leading past the Museum. The Museum is very instructive; time spent in sober reflection there is never wasted. One exhibit which usually exercises the minds of boys for many a long night is the one-armed teddy bear (Mr Wuggle) used by Croydon Minimus to inhume the Baron von Wedeltreppe-Steckenpferd in 1687. Since that fateful day, the Wendeltreppe-Steckenpferds have never allowed any soft toys within twenty miles of their castle in Uberwald.

78

Beyond the Museum, we reach Big School, which used to be the Guild's only classroom. It now serves principally as the Banqueting Hall and is also used for indoor sports, assemblies and examinations. Big School is the oldest unaltered room in College and its beams, despite their inaccessibility, have been carved with the names of most of the Guild's most famous Old Boys.

Just before the multi-denominational Chapel, there is a small door leading up to the bell tower, which houses the Inhumation Bell. This tolls the hours but, as befits the City's principal academy, it is always fashionably late. It also is tolled whenever news comes through of an Assassin successfully completing an assignment or upon the death of an old pupil of the college. Of course, this may quite often be one and the same event.

Proceeding further round we come to Liming Corridor which leads past Mr Wilkinson's Study to the Library. This is believed to be the largest Ankh-Morpork library outside Unseen University and, in the areas of assassination and other life-threatening professions, we like to think that it exceeds even UU's holdings of relevant tomes.

The Guild extends to five floors, excluding basements, dormer levels and lofts. The best way to explore the rest is as opportunities permit! Much of the building is out of bounds but, as Lord Downey would say, 'No one became a great Assassin by always obeying the rules. Of course, no one ever became a great Assassin by disobeying the rules *and getting caught*, either.'

At some time in their career, every pupil will see the inside of the Master of Assassins' study. Some will go for a cup of tea, a chat and the automatic avoidance of an almond slice, some will be going for a punishment, some will have been sent up for good, some will be going to receive bad news. In most cases they will not therefore be in a frame of mind to take in the details, but these are worth noting as the room is a classic example of a Guild study.

Impressive, oak-panelled and well-carpeted, it also serves as the Guild Council Chamber. Indeed, to one side you will see the Council's long, mahogany table. The room also contains the Master's own library and workbench – and who knows what mysterious substances may be stored in the dozens of intriguing drawers in his apothecary cabinet?

The study is dominated by the four huge black granite pillars that support the ornate ceiling. Four-square between those pillars, carved as they are with the names of famous Assassins, is the Master's desk, with its wrought-iron rack for birches and canes. These are a relic of the old days. In the modern college, we do not believe in anything so namby-pamby as corporal punishment.

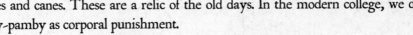

A HISTORY
OF THE GUILD

Classically, assassination as a profession began in the more mountainous regions of Klatch, where aspirants would partake of a drug known as *hasheesh* which, in sufficient quantities, would cause them to wear flared trousers and listen to really monotonous music with every sign of enjoyment.

Those early 'assassins' then disappeared into history and emerged somewhat later in the form we now recognise. Possibly their source of supply dried up.

The Guild as it exists today owes a great debt to its founders, Sir Gyles and Lady de Murforte. Sir Gyles was a warrior knight in the days of King Cirone I (Cirone the Unsteady). He quested extensively in Klatch for the greater glory of gold and, during one of his longer crusades against any Klatchians who had money, he learned of the brotherhood of assassins. At this time they were practising their craft for general hire and were already playing an important role in the internal politics of the Komplezianne Empire, rulers of Klatch at that time.[1] He was so impressed by the skill, poise, intelligence and wit of those Klatchian assassins whom he met (socially) that, far-sighted man that he was, he vowed to form a school for assassins in his native Ankh-Morpork. It was recorded by his clerk that his actual words were 'Onne daye we will neede to beat thys barstads atte theyre owne game.'

On his return to the city, he talked of his plans with his wife Lady de Murforte. She wholeheartedly supported her husband and he altered his will to leave most of his lands on the Sto Plains and many valuable sites in Ankh-Morpork for its construction.

Work on the new school began in 1511. Tutors were brought in from Klatch to train the city's brighter academics and psychopaths in the various skills needed to be a great assassin, so that the faculty should be ready when the building works had been completed. The old building on the site of the current Guild building had been a warehouse for scrolls and books and it was demolished so that a new, light, airy edifice could be erected to reflect the glory of the new school.

---

1 *The byzantine and convoluted politics of that lost Empire, which ruled from the now-buried city of Komplez, in fact were responsible for our word 'complex'.*

The de Murforte School for Gentlemen Assassins was officially opened by King Cirone II on 27 August 1512. Its first Head Master was Doctor Guillaume de Chacal. Dr de Chacal was not himself known to be an Assassin, but had been recruited direct from the prestigious Academie Quirmienne, where his reputation as a strict disciplinarian and moral leader was second to none, if one ignores a few wild accusations by people who were never able to produce any hard evidence.

The school then had 8 tutors and 72 students, known as King's Scholars. (The King had bestowed the Royal Charter on the school, together with a modest sum to fund the purchase of textbooks, weaponry and anatomical charts. The first influx of students also, as it happened, included Cirone, Prince of Llamedos, his eldest son.) All the students were then housed within the Guild building, in dormitories, or houses in the area which were then named simply after their key code on the architect's plans for the school.

Within a few years, the combination of royal patronage and the excellent standard of exam results being achieved by the now Royal de Murforte School for Gentlemen Assassins, had led to pressure from the city's wealthier inhabitants for its doors to be opened to students who, whilst they would benefit from the high standard of education available at the School, might not actually intend to kill people for a living. The King agreed to this extension to the School's charter and places were allocated to 24 children of citizens. These students were known as 'Oppidans', from the Latatian for 'town'.

81

The School went from strength to strength. Over the years, its numbers of students and staff rose, and boys were boarded in houses off-site, run by a number of women known as 'dames' because of a then-current tradition of wearing huge white drawers with red spots on and owning a dancing cow.

In 1576, the School was invited by the city's elders to elevate its status to that of a Guild, giving it voting rights in the city's Guild Council. It then changed its name to the Royal Guild of Assassins but, following the events of 1688, it wisely dropped the use of the 'Royal' from its title and restyled itself the Guild of Assassins.

Regrettably, in 1767, following a rash wager by the then head of the Guild, who believed that two pairs could beat any other hand, the freehold of the main Guild premises passed seamlessly to Sir John 'Mad Jack' Ramkin, and has remained in the possession of the Ramkin family until recently, when it became part of the marriage gift of Lady Sybil Ramkin to Sir Samuel Vimes, later His Grace the Duke of Ankh, with whom the Guild has a good working relationship.

It now has the original 72 King's Scholars (as they are still known) plus 180 Oppidans and a varying number of scholarship boys, the number of the latter usually decreasing as the term progresses. In this form it has continued to grow in reputation and influence in Ankh-Morpork and throughout the known Disc. Indeed, so great is the reputation of the Guild education that a number of students now come from Klatch.

There are many stories of Assassins meeting, in the course of business, clients who themselves were 'old boys' of the school, and singing a few verses of the old school song together before the inhumation was completed. There have been occasions where the client, shedding tears of joy at the fact that his death would be a part of the ancient and wonderful tradition, signed over a large part of his fortune to the Guild, and many Guild scholarships and bursaries are a result of this.

And of course all young Assassins know the story of Sir Bernard Selachii who, upon meeting an Assassin financed by a business rival, spent the entire evening with him, reminiscing about the great days they had shared in Wigblock House, before suggesting that they drink a toast to the old school and then, while his would-be assassin held his glass aloft, beating him to death with the brandy bottle. Subsequently Sir Bernard endowed the Sir Bernard Selachii Award for Sheer Coolth, a much coveted prize to this day.

SCHOOL PRIZES AND AWARDS

SENDING UP FOR GOOD

Despite its name, this is a good thing: it means you have produced a piece of schoolwork - practical or written - which is deemed by your tutor to be so outstanding as to merit your being sent up to the Master of Assassins' study for sherry and an almond slice. Your name is also then featured in the School Magazine. However, if you accept the almond slice, it will be in the obituary section - in CS we test, test and test again!

THE TEATIME PRIZE

This will be given after the Hogswatch and de Murforte Vacations for the two best Papers on the subject 'Who I Killed on My Holidays'. Pupils are not, of course, expected to actually *inhume* anybody, but a team of senior Assassins will assess the pupils' maps, routes, amassed information, professed target and projected methods of 'solution' before awarding the prize for the best *virtual* inhumation.

The prize is named after the late Noel Teatime, a young Assassin whose plans for the inhumation of Death, the Hogfather, the Soul Cake Duck, Old Man Trouble and several major gods were the talk of the Guild. His body has never been found.

THE INSIDIAE PLATE

Presented on Founder's Day by the Provost of Assassins. The winner is the constructor of the most elaborate trap mechanism in the Show and Tell section at Open Day, although actual killing will result in disqualification.

DISTINCTION IN TRIALS

Given to the top three boys in every year at end of term Trials (exams).

THE VENEFICUS CHALICE

Traditionally awarded at Gaudy Night to the pupil adjudged by the Head of Necrotic Medicine and Applied Pathology to have shown most promise in practical exercises in that specialism.

THE BODY TROPHY

Named after our popular old Under Master, Mr Wilberforce Body, this is awarded to the winning Team at the Wall Game.

THE BLANKMAN DIVINITY PRIZE

This is open to all boys in the Second and Third Years for the most realistic representation of the god of their choice achieved using only stale bread and sesame seeds.

THE ARS PLUMARIA CUP

This is won by the pupil scoring highest marks for Personal Grooming. A much-contested award.

THE WILKINSON CUP

Awarded annually to the boy who scores most consistently high marks at Fencing.

THE PENDU ILLUMINATED MANUSCRIPT

Awarded to the boy who wins the Climbing Competition at the Sports Day. The award is simply placed atop some high building in the city, and the pupil who returns to the Guild with it is adjudged the winner. The opportunities for waylaying, trapping, ambushing and cheating make this a remarkable exercise in Assassin skills.

THE PRACTICE OF ASSASSINATION:
THE RULES

(EXTRACT FROM THE 'NOBLE ART', BY LORD DOWNEY, MA)

Being aware that there must be some distinction between the Assassin and the common-murderer-for-pay which extends beyond the mere size of the payment involved, the Guild has evolved over the years a number of rules to govern the craft and prevent affairs from turning into an unseemly brawl.

In short, they are as follows:

- *An Assassin will not accept a contract on anyone who is unable to defend themselves, and collateral damage to bystanders, servants, etc., is considered extremely bad form.*

- *An Assassin is forbidden on pain of expulsion and instant clienthood from utilising any weapon of what we may guardedly call a firework nature. An Assassin uses skill and discipline, not alchemical contrivances. However, in certain circumstances compressed air has much to recommend it.*

- *Any adult who is in control of assets worth more than ten thousand dollars a year is considered able to defend themselves, or at least to employ someone to do it for them. It is not our fault if they do not. There is no helping some people.*

- *An Assassin will use only weapons that rely on his or her own strength, albeit in stored form. Thus, any kind of bow is acceptable, as is, say, a lead weight lifted and carefully placed over a door. Swords, knives, clubs, ropes and so on go without saying.*

- *An Assassin may also use an item that is merely moved from one place to another, as it might be a bucket of piranha fish, an electrical carpet or a chemical substance.*

- *Finally, an Assassin will only use those means which a client, if they are suitably wary and diligent, may detect and avoid. There is no honour in shooting someone from a distance in the street. The thoughtful and careful client must always have a chance. A man who cannot be bothered to test his shaving soap for poison every morning has lost the will to live.*

84

These rules apply only within Civilization, which is defined as the Sto Plains, most of the Ramtop Kingdoms, Genua and parts of Klatch.

SURVIVING YOUR FIRST FEW WEEKS

C.S. has been going now for centuries and there are many expressions and names for things that exist only in the oral tradition of the school. You may find it helpful to understand some of them; failing to do so may result in small yet painful ad hoc punishments, often involving the small hairs on the back of the hand.

SNOUT Head Master

BIG SCHOOL PREP Period in the evening when students can read, work or do hobbies (not involving weaponry)

BRICK Appreciative term for a boy skilled in wall climbing, one of the classic Assassin skills; *also* to take part in the inter-house edificeering competitions, when a boy might 'Brick for his House'. The name, of course, refers to the fact that a skilled climber might appear to those below to be just another brick in the wall

BUNKER A boy who's spent all his 'orno' and is unable to get 'sock'

SLAB A student's desk in his 'pit'

CRABS . . . and **CROAKERS, BUZZERS, SEEN'EMALLS, LOONIES, SLIDERS, FLAT'EADS, SOAPIES, BEDDIBOYS, RAGGIES, WIGGIES, RATS, SCARECROWS, TUMPERS, POPPIES** All semi-formal (that is to say, hallowed by time) nicknames for the various School Houses. We regret to say that the new Black Widow House has already attracted a number of nicknames, all of them unprintable except possibly for 'Darners' (because 'they'll all end up as Seamstresses one day', according to one little lad). Ah, the inventiveness of young manhood in its prime!

DRAINO A boy congenitally unskilled at climbing; by derivation, any unpopular person

EDIFICEERING, EDIFICEER, 'TO EDDY' Making one's way across a building or a large part of the city without ever touching the ground. A traditional Assassin skill, now often pursued as a pure sport

I think it may be time to reconsider some aspects of this, what with one thing and another. Especially the warming of beds.

✳ FAGGING Acting as servant to fifth- and sixth-formers; warming beds, making toast, taking messages

INHUMER, THE The Guild Magazine

LAST GASP, THE Nickname for the Guild Magazine

LISTS End of term assembly

LOFTING A fine Guild tradition and, to some extent, also a sport. Pupils of each House build, on the rooftops of the Guild or nearby, an eyrie or 'lofting', which may be a small shed or some more esoteric construction (the hanging 'weaver bird' lofting of Wigblock House was something of a city landmark for many years until its unfortunate collapse). They are used for initiation rites and the storage of House trophies. Typically, access is extremely difficult, and only available to a skilled edificeer. By strict tradition, no materials for lofting construction may be bought; they are generally scrounged, found, begged or stolen from the loftings of other houses.

Naturally, the loftings are a target for boys from the other Houses and also from the Thieves' Guild, traditional rivals. This leads to healthy competition and a state of permanent rooftop warfare, strike and counterstrike, raid and counter-raid, which in the opinion of some senior Assassins is worth a lifetime of classroom theory. A small trophy, the Roary Pig, is awarded annually by a committee of seniors. On those occasions when it is stolen by pupils from the Thieves' Guild, no members of the lofting last in possession are allowed beer with their meals for six months.

OPPIDAN Originally, a pupil drawn from the population of the city. Now used for any student not studying with intent to become a full Guild member

ORNO Pocket money sent from home, often entrusted to travelling bands of dwarfs

PILLS Poison, and by derivation, slang for Alchemy lessons and the Alchemy Master himself

PIT Student's study

PENNY READING The annual school play (from the days when the Senior Prefect could charge a penny a head to fund the provision of entertainment for the students)

PREFECT Sixth-form boys appointed by the Head Master; they keep records of boys who are late, untidy, dirty or dead, they are in charge of dormitories and can give certain punishments for infringements of the school rules. Prefects are allowed to wear the coveted badge, to use the

Trumper stairway, and need not wear hats when in Town.

PREP Work assigned by the 'ushers' for completion during 'Big School Prep'

SCHOLAR A King's Scholar, or scholarship boy. One of the students originally provided with textbooks, two quill pens, a pound of ink black, two quartos of blotting paper, a twelve-inch ruler and a six-inch dagger from the beneficence of King Cirone II. These scholars are now selected by competitive examination on the 'revised tontine' or 'last man standing' system, and their fees are paid by the Guild or by various bequests. They can be recognised by the heavy black woollen gown which they have to wear at all times, even when swimming.

SCAG An untidy or unpopular boy

SCAGGISH Bad form, lower class

SLATS School Assembly, or 'pray, say and flay' (the order usually being an interdenominational prayer, school announcement, and the flogging of serious offenders)

SLURK, SLURKING, SLURKER The classic Assassin method of movement, which may be considered as 'slinking' but with style and flair. Movement without apparent effort or undue visibility

SNODDIE CAD A purveyor of snoddie from a street barrow

SNODDIE Cakes, sweets, pies, &c.

SPARKLERS, SPARKIES Sixth-formers, who are traditionally allowed a certain additional flamboyance to their dress

CLAMP'S Tea Shop in Filigree Street. Famous for its cream buns and home-made ginger beer

SPLAT To fall, usually fatally, while 'edificeering', and hence any failure, disappointment, expulsion, &c.

TALLBOY Member of a House edificeering society; by derivation an all-round good chap, and the opposite of a 'draino'

TARDY-BOOKS Books maintained by the Prefects to record boys who are late for lessons or whose 'prep' is late or who are themselves terminally late

TIMBRALLS The Guild's sports field – in a corner of Hide Park

TOWN Literally anywhere in the city that is not Guild property

USHER Master

TRADITIONS

TUMPERS

It quickly became a tradition for the whole Guild to process to the Tump, where the new boys would be sprinkled with salt to instill them with wit for their coming years at CS, 'sal' meaning both salt and wit, and puns being the lowest form of the latter. Later this became a means of raising funds for Guild charities. Every year on 12 January, boys from the school go out in pairs on to the streets of Ankh-Morpork. One carries a stoneware pot of salt, the other a leather drawstring purse. They accost passers-by and encourage them to make a donation to the Guild. When they receive money, the donor is given a pinch of salt and everyone feels embarrassed.

THE WALL GAME

To the unfamiliar, this appears to be a cross between urban rock-climbing, squash and actual bodily harm. It is traditionally played on the walls of the Guild's inner courtyard, but 'friendly' and practice games are played anywhere on Guild property when a wall has been adapted to mimic some of the original features (such as 'Old Mother Baggy's Washing Line', 'the Window Box', 'the Coke Heaps', 'the Wonky Drainpipe', 'the Place Where the Mortar is Rotten' and so on). Two teams of three a side are involved, playing with a small ball made of cork wrapped in leather bands. The rules are complex, points being scored by bouncing the ball off walls and opposing players, and only one member of any team may be below 100 inches from the ground at any time. Most games run into injury time, sometimes for ever.

PULLIS CORVORUM

On Soul Cake Tuesday, the Guild chef catches a young magpie and attaches it to a pancake which he then nails to one of the Guild doors, incanting: 'Pullis corvorum invocantibus eum'. The poor bird is then worried to death by first-year students. A small prize, as yet unclaimed for more than two hundred years, will go to the boy who comes up with a halfway logical explanation for this.

CHAPEL SNODDIE

The pews nearest to the high altar are occupied by the Guild's teaching staff. Immediately below them, the pews are reserved for the Prefects. Old Prefects by tradition leave small packets of almonds and raisins for their new colleagues. This is known as Chapel Snoddie. It is, of course, a ritualised test; anyone who would eat any old food found lying around wouldn't last a term.

MAY BLOSSOM DAY

On May Day, if the Master of Assassins gives permission and if the day is moist, the boys are permitted to rise early and collect boughs of May blossom in Hide Park and decorate with them the windows of their dormitories. The boys are, however, not allowed to get their feet wet. For the past ninety years, no boy has bothered to give it a try.

BULLYING

Bullying is not a problem at CS. We do not believe in training pupils in a protected, hot-house atmosphere. After the first few weeks all boys go armed according to their ability, and we find that in most cases a boy who is not yet skilled with the throwing knife may have a natural talent with the sword; curiously enough, the weakest and smallest boy may well be an inventive genius with poisons, and so on. After a few scuffles and the occasional inevitable fatality, we find that a careful politeness reigns amongst the surviving pupils.

THE FOLLOWING OCCASIONS OF 'ACCEPTABLE HORSEPLAY' ARE HALLOWED BY TIME AND TRADITION:

TOSSING

A New Bod and four or five heavy, leather-bound books are placed together in a large woollen blanket. Several older boys then grasp the hem of the blanket and toss the boy and books up into the air, chanting: 'Ibis ab excusso missus ad astra sago'. On 'sago', the blanket's occupant should be propelled upwards to try to hit the ceiling. Much fun can be had from the injuries caused by blows to the New Bod from the heavy books. It is considered very bad form for him to subsequently hunt down the other boys.

TOASTING

This consists of cutting bread into thick slices and crudely cooking them in front of an open fire.

The term did use to have another meaning, but that custom died out, along with four boys, when, in a spirit of boyish good humour, they attempted to 'toast' a new boy, Mr Noel Teatime. The carnage that followed was an instructive example of what can be achieved with enthusiasm, determination and the common human thumb.

TIEING

When a New Bod has gone to sleep in the dorm, several larger boys enter, tie a strong rope to his big toe and then drag him out of bed, down the corridors and out into the main quad (or street for extra-mural Houses). There the boy is stripped and tied to one of the statues (quad) or horse troughs (street). What larks.

PENNING

A pen is formed by placing four beds into a square. A New Bod is placed in the pen and several larger boys then stand on the beds and kick the New Bod around the pen. Much fun can be had by betting on how long he can remain conscious before another New Bod has to be brought in to replace him. The New Bod is allowed to fight back, and should take heart from the fact that the current Head of School, Victor Ludorum, outlasted his tormentors for three hours during his first 'penning', suffocating one with a pillow, stunning another with a bedknob and strangling three others with his pyjama cord.

THE COLLEGE TUTORS

1. The Extremely Reverend Dr A-Pox-Upon-Their-Houses Jenkins (*Religious Studies*)

2. Mr Moody (*Personal Grooming*)

3. Baron Strifenkanen (*Applied Pathology*)

4. Kompt de Yoyo (*Modern Languages and Music*)

5. Dr von Ubersetzer (*Ancient Languages*)

6. M. de Balourd (*Dance and Deportment*)

7. Mme les Deux-Épées (*Fencing and Edged Weaponry*)

8. Mr Linbury-Court (*History*)

9. Mr Lamister

10. Lord Downey (*Master of Assassins*)

11. Mr Mericet (*Under Master*)

12. Mr Bradlofrudd (*Physical Education*)

13. Miss Band (*Climbing, Traps, Locks*)

14. Miss Smith-Rhodes (*Domestic Science and Organic Poisons*)

15. Professor Stone (*Alchemy and Metalwork*)

16. Lady T'malia (*Political Expediency*)

17. Mr Graumunchen (*Geography*)

91

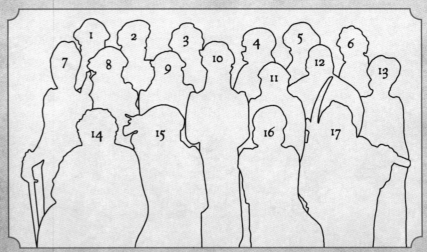

SCHOOL RULES

1. The whole of Filigree Street and (while boating is allowed) Frost Alley and Flood Walk is in bounds. The area around the Patrician's Palace is within bounds. The direct routes between the extra-mural Houses and the Guild building are in bounds for those times when boys are travelling between one and the other. All other parts of the city are out of bounds[1] without permission.

2. Boys are forbidden to enter any Theatre or Place of Public Entertainment, or Hotel, or Public House of any description, unless treating their House Tutor.

3. Boys are warned against playing card games with anyone calling themselves Doc or named after a geographical location or having a part of the body as a name, e.g., Doc Sharper, Pseudopolis Fats, Fingers McGee.

4. Boys are strictly forbidden from mentioning fruit within the hearing of the Matron.

5. Boys are warned against entering any Shops of a forbidden class, such as Tobacconists', Pawnbrokers', etc., as well as any that have been especially forbidden by the Head Master. They are also forbidden to enter any house of Ill-Repute; however, sixth-formers are allowed one (1) weekly visit to a house of Good Repute (an updated list is kept in the Porter's Lodge).

---

1 *Note: the definition of out of bounds is: 'a place where a pupil may not be seen by staff'. An Assassin will often need to spend time in places where he should not be, and this rule should supply valuable experience.*

6. Boys are expressly forbidden from teasing Mr Lamister.

7. Boys are strictly forbidden to buy or to have in their possession any Spirit, Fat or Mineral Oil, or any other inflammable or explosive material, or fireworks of any description.

8. Boys are not allowed to keep ungulates of any description in their rooms.

9. No boy is to whistle in the Combination Corridor during Mr Moody's lessons.

10. Boys are not allowed to walk around the Guild or the Town without their hands in their pockets.

11. Boys may not run in the corridors of the Guild.

12. Boys may not play at Ramcat in the Big School.

13. No boy is to make Huckle-My-Buff in his room.

14. Boys are strictly forbidden to use Mr Lamister's door as a target.

15. Boys may not wear vests for Sports.

∗16. No boy is to wear his hair longer than shoulder length.

17. By custom and practice, boys are allowed to carve their names once upon their desks and once upon the roof leads of Big School. Boys are emphatically not allowed to carve their initials on Mr Lamister's leg.

18. No boy is to keep a crocodile in his room.

18A. No boy is to keep an alligator or any large amphibious reptile in his room.

18B. No boy, we wish to make it clear, is to keep any kind of monitor, goanna or giant chameleon in their room.

18C. Nor in the cellar.

18D. Nor in a cage on the roof.

18E. No boy is to own, rent, lease or hire any kind of lizard, amphibian or any species of creature broadly resembling the aforesaid (dead or alive) in his room, or anywhere else on, in, above or under Guild premises, or in any dimension occasionally congruent with this one, nor is any boy allowed to keep an alligator (or similar) costume, or possess a humorous inflatable alligator (or similar) that may be dangled on the end of a string in front of the window of the study below. Pictures of crocodilians and related creatures of a size normally expected in a work on natural history are acceptable. Newts may be kept for the purposes of nature study.

18F. Boys are forbidden to keep any newt of any length greater than five (5) inches at full growth. Despite significant differences apparently visible to the educated eye, the Sumtri Fire Newt is defined as a crocodilian under School Rules, in so far as it is capable of eating a full-grown master.

93

∗ This rule may be relaxed if the boy is a girl.

18G. None of the above rules 18-18F applies to pupils who are worshippers of Offler the crocodile god.

18H. No boy is to convert to Offlerism without permission in writing from the Head Master.

18I. Any boy pretending Offlerism may, at the whim of the Head Master, be subjected to twenty complicated questions on its tenets and beliefs. Inaccuracy in this area will result in expulsion. Religion is not a joking matter.

18J. The Guild of Assassins and its associated teaching establishment fully accept that to the worshippers of Nog-Humpy the custard god, religion is a joking matter.

19. Any boy found at any time (apart from in bed) not in possession of two stiletto daggers and (boys over 4'9") a sword of suitable length, plus at least three approved concealed weapons (see list in Big School) will be expelled without appeal.

19B. Any girl found at any time (apart from in bed) without at least two stiletto daggers and three concealed weapons (see list in Matron's Office) will be expelled without appeal. Whilst aware that female clothing offers many opportunities for concealment, and whilst also aware that inventiveness should be encouraged, the following items are restricted to girls in year four and above:

    A. poisoned underthings of any description

    B. spring-loaded corsetry

20. Girls are reminded that Miss Band's 'Porcupine' elasticated bustle bombard, whilst undoubtedly effective, has been outlawed by the Guild Council for wear anywhere within five hundred miles of Ankh-Morpork.

21. Any boy not in possession of a valid sick note who cannot, at any time, within three seconds, have a pistol bow cocked and aimed and/or a sword at the ready, will be sent to the Head Master. This applies on a 24-hour basis (apart from Swimming).

22. Boys who favour the concealed cuff bow will, pending a Guild review of the use of this weapon, refrain from wearing it at mealtimes or other occasions where it may be necessary to pass things to other pupils.

23. Poison rings are to be placed in the receptacle provided before any pupil does Domestic Science.

24. No boy shall build a deadfall in his room.

When required, for boys read girls, and vice versa.

95

FURTHER SCHOOL RULES

137. No pupil is to attempt to assassinate any other pupil during morning prayers.

139. The use of contrivances powered by springs, elastic or other means for the automated writing of 'lines' is forbidden. The writing of lines for more fortunate pupils is traditionally the province of the Scholarship Boys, who are entitled to charge one penny per hundred words.

145. No boy is to enter the room of any girl.

146. No girl is to enter the room of any boy.

147. (provisional) It has been pointed out that our injunction to 'read boys for girls, and vice versa', can, if taken together with the two previous rules by someone with little to do but argue, mean that no pupil is to be in any room at all. This was not the intention. No pupil is to be anywhere except where they should be. A girl is defined as a young person of the female persuasion.

148. Regardless of how persuaded he feels, Jelks Minor in Form IV is a boy.

149. Arguing over the wording of school rules is forbidden.

150. Matters of a Delicate and/or Personal Nature may be discussed with Matron after tea on Tuesdays and Thursdays. Pupils must put their names on the list in Big School. Time-wasting with frivolous or irrelevant questions is punishable, as are anatomical questions of any description.

151. Lurking Behind The Stables: pupils not found lurking behind the stables at least once per term will be reprimanded; lurking is an essential skill and should be practised whenever possible. Pupils who can provide evidence that they were *in fact* lurking but were not spotted will be awarded a gold star on their report.

152. Boys are not allowed to slide down the coke heaps.

167. Whilst the Guild encourages improving hobbies of all kinds, the following pursuits are banned on Guild premises: 1) Taxidermy of animals over 6" long; 2) Tanning; 3) the Training of wild animals (with the exception of white mice and the Brindisian Yodelling Stick-insect).

169. No boy is allowed to grow a moustache until he is in the Sixth Form.

169A. In deference to the new arrangements, no girl is to grow a moustache until she is in the Sixth Form, either.

170. No pupil is to try to walk like Mr Lamister.

UNIFORM & EQUIPMENT

The correct clothing for any Assassin 'at large' is black; indeed, many Assassins wear no other colour even in their leisure hours, although deep purples and greys will not cause comment.

Boys are not allowed to wear black in their first two years, but may 'take dark' some time in their third year if they are making satisfactory progress.

Boys (under 5'6") in their first year at the Guild must wear the New Bod uniform of a midnight blue coat and knee breeches, worn with cream waistcoat and ruffled shirt, the whole capped off with a black tricorn of beaver pelt. New Bod Scholars wear white duck trousers instead of the knee breeches and, of course, their heavy woollen Scholar's gown.

Boys over 5'6" must wear all of the above plus a sheepish expression.

First- and second- year girls of any size must wear a black gymslip or pinafore, black woollen stockings, and round hat known as the 'blonker'.

The purpose of these outfits is to make the pupils feel rather foolish, and hence determined to succeed in their studies and 'take dark' at the earliest opportunity.

After 'taking dark', pupils are expected to dress fashionably whilst eschewing bright colours; young women are enjoined not to dress in a way that might unduly inflame the amorous propensities of their male colleagues. All pupils must wear the Guild's crest on their lapel.

All pupils pursuing post-graduate studies are entitled to dress and conduct themselves as full Assassins.

Note: Only Prefects may carry their umbrellas furled.

UNIFORM & EQUIPMENT ON ARRIVAL AT SCHOOL

In addition to the list of acceptable clothing, which all parents will have received separately, the following should be found in the trunk of any new arrival:

One pair of Woollen Gloves, with cord to go through coat

One Waterproof Rain Cape

Three Sets Clothes, Black (silk and/or velvet), for Practical exercises

One Broad-Brimmed Black Hat (with cheesewire – see below)

Hairnets (girls only)

One Assassins' Guild Scarf

Five Flannelette Nightshirts (for winter terms)

One Night Cap, humorous

One pair of Slippers, preferably in pastel colours and with an animal motif1

One knitted woollen Bathing Suit

One Sports Singlet

One Guild Dressing Gown

One Apron2, floral (Domestic Science)

One Apron, leather (Alchemy)

A soft felt roll containing Throwing Knives 1, 2, 4 & 5, plus Stiletto Knives in sizes AA, AB, AC and AD

No. 3 Throwing Knife in leather thigh sheath

No. 7 Pencil Eraser

One Junior Set, Throwing Tlingas

Thin Silk Line and Folding Grappling Hook

One Chain Mail Shirt (lightweight)

One Geometry Set containing Compasses, Protractor, Divider, Set Square

One Poison Set containing phials of Wasp Agaric, Achorion Purple & Mustick

One Set, Brass Knuckles

One Soft bag of Caltraps

One Rapier and Black Velvet Baldric

One Blowpipe, 12" & Tin of Darts, Cork-Tipped with Braille identification marks

One Slingshot and Lead Ammunition (Size 12)

One Pencil Case with H, HB, B & 2B Pencils, Small Eraser (size 1) & two Pens

One Pair, Armoured Gloves

One Pair, Armour-soled Shoes (Priests)

One Set, Crampons

One Set, Pitons (various)

One Chemistry Rag

Three Karabiners

One Universal Kit – Extendable Metal Rods with Attachments, including Mirror

One 18" Ruler, marked out in tenths and in sixteenths of an inch

One Portable Inkwell (pewter)

One pair, Diamond-tipped Compasses, in pouch

One Flask of Fine Oil

One Soft Leather Roll of Lock Picks

One Apron, Canvas, for Woodworking classes

One Punch Dagger

One Junior Alchemist's Kit – with phials of Copper Sulphate, Wood Chips and Sodium Bicarbonate

Two Burleigh & Stronginthearm 'Wasp' Foldaway Pistol Crossbows and Quarrels

Two Cheesewires, suitable for concealment in brim of Hat

98

---

1 *Not a rabbit design of any description for those boys in Cobra House or any other House to which Mr Lamister may be assigned.*
2 *Any boy or girl found with an apron decorated with an amusing torso or slogan such as 'Come And Get It While It's Hot' will be sent home.*

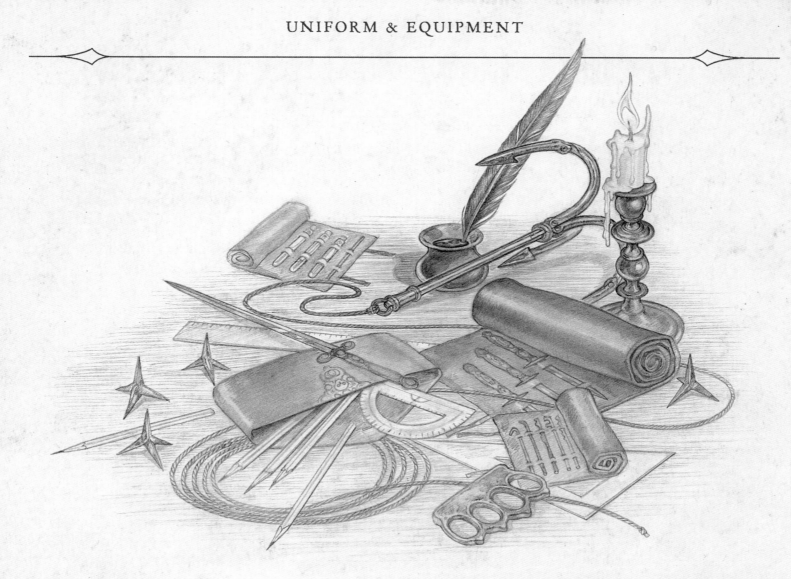

NOTES: It is a strict rule that *all* possessions must have a name tape sewn in, or the pupil's name die-stamped on the hilt, handle or other suitable place. This rule extends to arrows and slingshot ammunition. Cheesewires must be finished with a suitable metal label.

Some parents have queried whether or not pupils may be permitted to use blunted weapons and weapons made 'safe' by other means. Practice swords are used in initial fencing lessons. Beyond that, the Guild takes the view that 'pretend' weapons should only be used by pupils who expect to come up against artificial opponents. It is a deadly and dangerous world beyond the walls of the Guild, and it is up to us to see that it remains that way.

CONLEGIUM SICARIORUM

SCHOOL HOUSES

Viper House (Mr Nivor)

B2 House {day pupils} (Dr von Ubersetzer)

Scorpion House (Lady T'malia)

C1 House {day pupils} (Dr Perdore)

Tump House (Miss Band)

Mykkim House (Mr Linbury-Court)

Broken Moons House (Mr Moody)

Mrs Beddowe's House (M. le Balourd)

Raguineau's (Baron Strifenkanen)

Tree Frog House {day pupils} (Mr Bradlofrudd)

Pernypopax Dampier (Professor Stone)

BlackWidow House {girls} (Mme les Deux-Épées)

Cobra House (Mr Mericet)

Welcome Soap House (Mr Graumunchen)

WigBlock Prior (Kompt de Yoyo)

Raven House (Miss Smith-Rhodes)

GUILD OFFICERS

Provost of Assassins: Havelock, Lord Vetinari, DMAP, DM, DGS, MA, MPE, MASc, MIDD, BScI, DiPE

Master of Assassins (Head Tutor & Guild President): Lord Downy, MA

Under Master: Mr Mericet, DMAP, MA, BScI

Guild Tutors

Political Expediency: Lady T'malia, MA, MPE, BScI

Physical Education: Mr Bradlofrudd DiHI (Llamedos)

Fencing and Edged Weaponry: Madame les Deux-Épées, MA, DiPE

Traps and Advanced Ambush: Mr Nivor, MA, BScI

Ancient Languages: Doktor von Ubersetzer, DL

Dance and Deportment: Monsieur le Balourd, MIDD

Alchemy and Metalwork: Professor Stone, MASc

Applied Pathology: Baron Strifenkanen, DMAP

Personal Grooming: Mr Moody, BW

History: Mr Linbury-Court, MA

Modern Languages and Music: Kompt de Yoyo, DM, DL

Mathematics: Mr Schotter, MS

Geography: Mr Graumunchen, MA

Religious Studies / Chaplain: The Extremely Rev. Dr A-Pox-Upon-Their-Houses Jenkins, DGS

Climbing, Traps, Locks: Miss Band, DiPE

Domestic Science & Organic Poisons: Miss Smith-Rhodes

Guild Staff

Matron: Sister Lister, SSSHS

Scullion: Mr Robey

Bursar: Mr Winvoe, MGAU

Porter: Mr Stippler

College Porter: Mr Bracegirdle

Chef: Monsieur Insignes-Fovant, FGC

Head Brewer (hon.): Mr Bearhugger

Taster: (POSITION VACANT)

Chief Butler: Mr Carter, MGB

Student Officials

Captain of Assassins: Douglas, G.R.W.

Keepers of the Wall: Ludorum, V.; Egerton F.W.G

Captain of Scholars: Bastion, C.A.T.

Keeper of the Weapons: Bastion, C.A.T.; Jennings, J.C.T.

Captain of Oppidans: Jennings, J.C.T.

Chief Chronicker: Sotley, A.

Captain of Boats: Ludorum, V.

Head Dagswain: Grose, S.W.

Captain of Everything: Ludorum, V.

Holder of the Humboxes: Armsbury, K.

President of the Debating Society: Egerton, F.W.G.

Keepers of the Field: Douglas, G.R.W.; Ludorum, V.

DEGREES
(awarded both by the Guild and associated Guilds)

MA   Master Assassin

BW   Bachelor of Wig-making

MPE   Master of Political Expediency

DM   Doctor of Music

BScI   Bachelor of the Science of Inhumation

MS   Master of Sums

DiHI   Diploma of Homicidal Insanity

DGS   Doctor of Gods' Studies

DL   Doctor of Languages

SSSHS Spiteful Sister of Seven-Handed Sek

MIDD Member of the Institute of Dance & Deportment

MGAU Member of the Guild of Accountants and Usurers

DiPE   Diploma of Physical Education

MGB   Member of the Guild of Butlers

MASc Master of Alchemical Science

FGC   Fellow of the Guild of Chefs

DMAP Doctor of Medicine & Applied Pathology

FAMOUS INSTRUMENTS
OF DESPATCH

JEWELLERY

Lady T'malia (BlackWidow). Believed
to have enough poison concealed in the
jewellery of one hand alone to poison a
continent. Very few shake hands with her
and live to boast of it.

GRAPPLING HOOK

Mr Chidder (Viper) is believed to have
successfully completed his commission by
accidentally impaling the Baron von Falle
with his grappling iron whilst attempting to
gain entry to Schloß Blom.

MACKEREL

The Grand Vizier of El Sanlu (Wigblock Prior) stabbed to death the Emir of El Kaound with a frozen mackerel at a dried-up oasis in the middle of the Great Nef, the Discworld's hottest and driest desert. The Grand Vizier then died of wounds from a blow from, apparently, a live turbot. There are many aspects of this fight which remain a mystery.

WALLPAPER

One of the Emperors of Brindisi was inhumed by Dr de Colleuse (Viper). Dr de Colleuse had planned to inhume him by using poisoned wallpaper in the state bedroom. He was, however, discovered in the act and with great initiative, clubbed the Emperor to death with one of the rolls of paper.

POISONED SWEETS

All students are warned against accepting sweets from strangers or from Lord Downey (Mrs Beddowe's).

MOLE

Sir Guy de Taupinier (Viper) had been commissioned to assassinate King Guillaume le Rouge. Seizing an opportunity during a deer hunt in the Royal Forest, Sir Guy used a catapult to propel a dead mole (found along the wayside) at the King, which knocked him from his horse, causing him to break his neck and die.

A COMMON TEASPOON

Wielded by the Hon. Stanley Cabshaw against a group of bandits on the Quirm road (a government contract). Details are sketchy, and perhaps this is just as well.

HORSEHAIR SOFA

Lady Prill (Viper) came up with this innovate method to dispose of the Moon King of Brindisi. She impregnated the horsehair with the venom of the Tezuman Tree Frog. When the King sat on the sofa, the horsehair penetrated the skin of his legs and he died within seconds.

SLEDGEHAMMER

F.D.R. Mason (Mykkim) was the first Assassin to undertake a commission against a troll, attempting to despatch Mr Marble by hitting him over the head with a sledgehammer outside an inn in the Shades. Mr Mason's eventual return to the Guild was slightly marred by his being pushed under the main door. Students returning from an evening's drinking mistook him for an ornamental doormat and his fate was not discovered until morning.

106

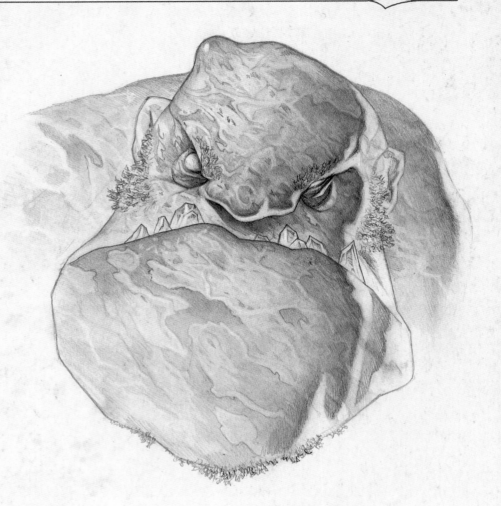

A BUTT OF BRANDY

On a commission from the late Duke of Sto Helit, Mr R.P.W. Roberston (Pernypopax Dampier) inhumed the Duke of Sto Kerrig by drowning him in a barrel of best brandy. By a terrible accident, the sealed butt was later bought by the Guild, and for some months members commented upon the interesting smoky flavour. It was only when the dye from the Duke's jacket turned the brandy green that the lid was levered up and he was found, perfectly preserved and smiling . . .

EXPLODING PRIVY

This was used by Mr Trefor Frame against Mr Edwin Cardly at a coaching inn in Slake. It was a matter of opportunity, a more elaborate death having been planned further along the road, but Mr Frame said 'It suddenly dawned on me that all I need do was throw my lighted cigar with extreme accuracy.'

MISS ALICE BAND'S
EXPLODING BUSTLE

KEY

A. Miss Band

B. Bustle on wicker frame; space below easily accommodates additional weaponry in case of Eventualities

C. 'Falchion' Compressed Air Device, lethal in a ten-yard radius

D. Adjustable Timer Mechanism to allow swift yet ladylike departure

E. Hidden pedal-operated Release Mechanism and primer

GUILD COMMISSIONS

HAROLD, DUKE OF PSEUDOPOLIS

Rather messily, with a cudgel, length of chain, pistol crossbow, dagger, poison and, ultimately, by the attachment of an anchor and immersion in water by Prince Podgourny (not a Guild member). His Grace the Duke was a man of iron constitution and took some considerable time to be persuaded to give up. Prince Podgourny in the end had to drag the still struggling Duke to the nearby frozen river, hack a hole in the ice and then shove him in. The Prince caught a chill as a result and died three months later.

OLERVE THE BASTARD, KING OF STO LAT

Cleanly, with a crossbow, by Guillaume Dire (Pernypopax Dampier). Regrettably, this Old Boy was found poisoned two days after this commission was completed. It is believed that he was himself inhumed by his employer. This is always a possibility, and student Assassins are warned against accepting gifts of food or hospitality before the fee has been banked.

KANG, LORD OF AGATEA

Swiftly, with a jigsaw puzzle, by H.K. Smarter (Viper). This one remains a mystery as Mr Smarter took the methodology with him to his grave.

'BOGEY BOB'

One of Ankh-Morpork's vagrant community, he was killed by having a table nailed to his head by an unknown Assassin, who nevertheless left a receipt with an indecipherable signature. An appalling example of poor gamesmanship, and almost certain not to be the work of a real Guild member.

JULIAN I, EMPEROR OF TSORT

One of a thankfully few mass assassinations. Several Members had separately decided to go for the fairly large purse being offered by the then Empress of Tsort. In the event his bedroom was invaded at dead of night by Messrs Cascara (Scorpion), Cassawary (Mrs Beddowe's), Parmensis (Pernypopax Dampier) and Quintas (Viper), who each took an independent route and all, in the darkness, mistook one another for guards. Apparently the Emperor slept through the whole thing. This was an embarrassment to the Guild and the system was changed to avoid recurrences.

PATRICIO, DESPOT OF QUIRM

The Guild's largest client, at 43 stone. A team led by senior Assassin Lord Robert Selachii (Scorpion) and Mr Sendivoge (Welcome Soap) inhumed the Despot, with a break for lunch.

COUNT DRAGOUL VON SALIC, OF UBERWALD

The Count was successfully inhumed by four separate generations of the same family - J.C.R. Wiggs, his son P.M.T. Wiggs, his grandson S.T.D. Wiggs and his great-grandson B.S.E. Wiggs (all of Viper). The Count is currently back on the Open Commissions List, and by general agreement will remain so until Miss Jocasta Wiggs graduates from the Guild.

OPEN COMMISSIONS

HAVELOCK, LORD VETINARI
AM$1M

Lord Vetinari is himself a graduate of the Guild and as such is a formidable opponent. Whilst he is known to view assassination attempts as a normal part of his life as a politician, and whilst he fully understands that the Guild's members are obliged to take on such commissions, he nevertheless takes a firm view that a dog only gets one bite. Most of the Assassins who have tried to earn the AM$1,000,000 fee have never been heard of since.

III

RINCEWIND (ASSISTANT LIBRARIAN AT UU)
—— AM$950K ——

Mr Rincewind is one of nature's survivors. He seems not to be a violent man, but Assassins attempting this commission seem to find themselves the victims of unexplained accidents - falling slates, lightning strikes - or, and this is worth noting, being waylaid by Mr Rincewind's travel accessory.

112

CMDR VIMES
—— AM$600,000, AND RISING ——

Cmdr Vimes rather irritatingly takes it all in good part. Many attempts have been made and the Assassins have, in the main, returned in one piece (albeit slightly singed, or painted yellow, or limping). Cmdr Vimes does not play by the rules - any rules.

113

THE DUCK MAN
— AM$132K —

Despite the large reward, no Assassin has yet attempted this one. Everyone is too intrigued by this bizarre commission. The identity of the person behind this offer has never been revealed.

114

CORPORAL 'NOBBY' NOBBS
—— AM$4.31 ——

This one is believed to be a joke perpetrated by Cpl Nobbs' Watch colleagues. Cmdr Vimes has let it be known that he would be 'upset' if this commission were to be carried out.

FOUL OLE RON
— ONE GROAT —

No Assassin has been sufficiently mindless of his personal reputation to take this job. It is certainly doubtful that Mr Ron's peculiar pungency would allow any method short of an extremely accurate long-distance bowshot.

MEMBERS OF STAFF

PROFESSOR STONE
Alchemy and Metalwork

Professor Stone is the inventor of many of the Guild's more recent weapons, such as the tiny one-shot crossbow, concealed palm dagger and a whole range of devious jewellery. Pupils should enter his workshop with more than usual care, and be careful what they touch. Testing is not just for exams; testing is for life!

117

THE EXTREMELY REV. DR A-POX-UPON-THEIR-HOUSES JENKINS
Religious Studies

Although of the Omnian persuasion, the Rev. Jenkins is a practitioner of many other religions and says he is quite happy to believe anything. A speciality subject of his is hand-to-hand Smiting – not just hip and thigh, but at many little-known bones and muscles.

118

BARON STRIFENKANEN
Applied Pathology

The Baron is very much a 'character' of the Guild, and the pupils certainly enjoy his amusing practical jokes and demonstrations of ventriloquism . . .

MISS ALICE BAND

Climbing, Traps, Locks, also private tuition in Stealth Archaeology, Pistol Bow, Croquet and Pianoforte

Miss Band has had a distinguished career at the more robust end of education, and her introduction of Free-Form Hockey to the Quirm College for Young Ladies is unlikely to be forgotten. Any senior pupils wishing to take (as she puts it) 'liberties' will be taught a lesson they will remember for the rest of their lives; they will not need long memories.

120

MR GRAUMUNCHEN
Geography ('You can't kill 'em, boyo, if you can't find 'em!')

Considers applied Geography to be a vital Assassin skill, and even runs special courses on flint knapping and obsidian working so that no Guild member, however extreme his circumstances, need be short of an edge. He is extremely proud of being one of the first dwarfs born in Ankh-Morpork, prouder still that he has never been down a mine, and declares that he wouldn't think of hitting a rock with anything bigger than a small hammer.

FAMOUS OLD BOYS

JOHAN LUDORUM (VIPER)

One of the greatest Assassins in the history of the Guild. Responsible for twelve royal inhumations. His son, Victor Ludorum (Viper), is following in his father's footsteps as a post-graduate and has already seen off two Princes and a Regent during the holidays.

ZLORF FLANNELFOOT (C1)

Past President of the Guild. Mr Flannelfoot is the only Assassin in recent years to have risen to high office from low birth. Not a fast thinker in academic matters, he did have a good grasp of the principle of 'dead men's shoes'. Very badly scarred, giving people the impression that someone has been trying to cross out his face.

PTEPPICYMONXXXXX
(VIPER)

Son of the Pharoah of Djelibeybi,
Pteppic passed with flying colours.
His current whereabouts are unknown.

123

'71-HOUR' AHMED (VIPER)

Better known to Old Sicarians as Ahmed the Bed-Wetter. Ahmed is now the head of the Klatchian Police, reporting direct to Prince Khufurah. Although Ahmed does technically spend much of his time killing people for money, he no longer undertakes Guild commissions as such.

CHARLES H.J. WIGGS (WIGBLOCK PRIOR)

Of the famous Guild family, he never actually worked as an Assassin, having been blown from the roof of the Guild whilst returning to his study after taking his final examination in hurricane conditions. He was awarded an honorary pass and his parting was commemorated by his father by the commissioning of the weather vane which even now adorns the Guild.

DISGRACED OLD BOYS

JULIAN FLIEMOE (TREE FROG)

Abully and a liar, Fliemoe seemed ideally suited to his chosen profession, but he never achieved success, being an unbelievable liar and an unsuccessful bully. Mr Fliemoe was transferred to the Guild of Lawyers where these character traits worked to his advantage.

EDWARD D'EATH (VIPER)

Not only did Edward kill without a valid commission but also, and more importantly, he stole Guild property. Unforgivable.

128

MR TEATIME (B2)

Mr Teatime failed to carry out a major commission for which the Guild had been paid a very large sum of money indeed. Also, his essay, 'Who I Killed on My Holidays', is considered to be a pathetic flight of juvenile imagination copied from a work of fiction in the Guild library, *Decem Parvi Indi*.

129

DR CRUCES (TREE FROG)

Not only did Dr Cruces fail dismally to complete the open commission on Lord Vetinari, but he also murdered an Old Sicarian and a member of the City Watch (that is to say, he killed without payment). Not a good example to younger Assassins.

GRAV DRAC VON GLOCKEN, DRAGON KING OF ARMS (B2)

He designed the Guild's coat of arms and was also responsible for its motto. His own escutcheon was irrevocably blotted, though, when he was implicated in the circumstances surrounding a number of unpaid-for-deaths in the city. Current whereabouts uncertain.

130

MAKING CRIME PAY WITH
THE THIEVES' GUILD

Terry reignited in me a shared interest in the trivia of history. We were both fascinated by the discovery of undiscovered trifles (not the dessert). Having been a frankly lazy schoolboy, I found to my surprise that I relished the 'work' of researching the history of crime and punishment, and constructing on Discworld little hidden echoes of roundworld institutions, such as (for example) the use of 'clink' as a word for gaol.

STEPHEN BRIGGS

This series of drawings was largely influenced by the Victorian criminologist and photographer, Alphonse Bertillon, who was dubbed 'father of the mugshot'. His images show a fine array of lamb-chop facial hair, shifty eyes and heavy brows - features that pair perfectly with the ne'er-do-wells of the Ankh-Morpork underworld.

PAUL KIDBY

One of the remarkable innovations introduced by the Patrician was to make the Thieves' Guild responsible for theft, with annual budgets, forward planning and, above all, rigid job protection. Thus, in return for an agreed average level of crime per annum, the thieves themselves saw to it that unauthorised crime was met with the full force of Injustice, which was generally a stick with nails in it.

TERRY PRATCHETT

ACVTVS ID VERBERAT

THIEVES'

GUILD

136

The President's Address

It is with a great deal of pleasure that I dictate this the introductry paragraph for the first Yearbook for the Ankh-Morpork Guild of Thieves. It is not so long ago that our Guild wouldn't have had enough literit members to make a book like this worthwhile. Now all the other Guilds are doin it anyway and we can't let everyone think we can't put crayon to paper eh Harry don't put that bit in.

This has been a difficult year for our ancient Guild as we have tried to come to terms with various new business chalenges. Let me say first and foremost I want to make it clear that I am not the one to rake over old wounds. Many harsh words have been uttered. We have lost many new friends during the protracted discussions. Some of our members who are banged up in the Tanty have had so much compassionate time off to attend funerals that its not been worth them going back at night time, also it is becoming so hard to hire the proper big black hearses with the plumes and everything that sometimes funerals have had to be arranged several months in advance, ha ha which can come expensive if the would-be deceased legs it in the meantime don't put that in Harry.

At this point I would like to repeat once more how personally gutted I was to hear of the serious smacking of Herbert 'Shady' Shover and his friends in Mobson's Livery Stable on Soul Cake Tuesday last. I make no secret of the fact that Herbert and I did not see eye to eye on many issues and I know he publicly called me 'a daft old wally who thinks thieves still ort to wear stripey jumpers' but I laughed this off as the Folly of Youth. Persnally I thought there was a lot of merit in his ideas, such as the wearing of black suits at all times also dark glasses, but this is Not The Time. As everyone knows my lady wife Vi and myself sent the largest wreath to the funeral and I cried for hours. We shall not see Herbert's like again ha ha or several of his fingers I heard don't put that bit in Harry.

But now is a time for reconciliation, and I hope this book will serve to prove once again that we of the Guild are, dispite all our diferences, one big happy Family.

J.H. Boggis (Mr)

dictated to Harry ('Can't Remember His Nickname') Jones, Guild Secretary.

From Lord Vetinari

I am very pleased to be able to pen these few lines to celebrate the 21st anniversary of the founding of the Guild of Thieves. What a time it has been, indeed. I can say, in all honesty, that Mr Boggis and his fellow Guild leaders have been everything I could have expected of them.

Newcomers to Ankh-Morpork say to me: 'Is crime here really *legal?*' And the answer is: Yes, but it depends on the crime. Crimes against the person unconnected with the passage of goods or money are certainly *not* legal. There is no logic to them. And vandalism I regard as an extremely serious crime: theft is merely a disagreement over ownership, whereas vandalism is a denial of the very principle of property. Happily, most crimes simply involve the movement of goods, and as such can be regulated.

When I became ruler of the city, upon the sudden demise of the late Lord Snapcase, unregulated gangs of criminals still dominated many areas. Their methods were often violent and erratic. Crime was random and unfair. It was, in a word, disorganised. How much better, then, to encourage the major gangs to combine and incorporate into the Guild we know today.

The end of crime? Impossible. But once upon a time taxation was a matter of arriving in an area with a lot of soldiers and shaking the citizens by their heels until you had enough money or, failing that, teeth. Now the formal demanding and payment of city taxes is accepted as the price of living in a city and, of course, of not being beaten senseless by soldiers. Seen in the correct light, crime is merely a kind of taxation, which, as I have indicated, is itself only a sophisticated version of 'demanding money with menaces'.

What people fear is randomness. What people fear is chaos. The Guild represents order. Seen in the light of reality, everyone gains. Theft continues, yes, but under control and often by arrangement. The fear is removed from the equation. In addition, the Guild also removes from the hard-pressed City Watch the need to police against property crime. The Guild sticks rigorously to an annual budget, and deals strictly with members and non-members who exceed it. Very strictly, I am pleased to say.

And thus everyone is happy or, more correctly, no one worth worrying about is *too* unhappy, substantial amounts of fear and uncertainty are removed from the lives of many, and money circulates rapidly, which is always a good thing. It is hard to see what more can be hoped for, in this imperfect world.

In a spirit of fraternal goodwill, may I on this occasion sign myself

Havelock 'Do Not Let Me Detain You' Vetinari

138

TREASURER'S REPORT

REAL FAMILY VALUES

by Vinny 'No Ears' Ludd

In these troubled times – and it is amazing how quickly times you think are peaceful can turn into troubled times, believe me, especially in the vicinity of Willie Hobson's Livery Stable – it is well worth bearing in mind that what the Guild stands for above all is Reliability, Tradition and Service.

There has been some grumbling this year about Guild activities and changes in the Budget, and some people have been saying perhaps the city can do without the Thieves' Guild at all. We have the Watch, they say.

Crime is always with us – well, not with us, as such, obviously, but with civilisation in general – and we owe it to Lord Vetinari for pointing out that, since this is the case, it could be done better.

And we do it better. And we do it *reliably*. And we do it *traditionally*.

Look at the situation in those cities that do not have Guilds. People don't know when they are going to be robbed. They don't know how much will be taken. They live in fear of crime rather than, as in Ankh-Morpork, accepting it as a kind of goods-and-services tax. Why is this? Because they are in the hands of *amateurs*.

Take your non-Guild burglar, for example. What does he know about skilled lock picking? Or casing the joint? About being quiet? Nothing. He smashes a window, turns out all the drawers, rummages around where he shouldn't . . . and that's only the start of your problems.

How often have you heard people say, 'I wouldn't've minded, they didn't take much, but the *mess*!' That's not the work of a Guild burglar! Usually people will not find out they've been robbed until the lady next looks for her necklace and finds only our receipt in the box. A Guild burglar takes pride in his work. In fact, some of our clients have been so kind as to inform us that the only reason they suspected a break-in was when they saw that the dressing table had been dusted and the cat had been fed.

The same applies to street crime. Your non-Guild mugger, now, what does he know about anatomy? Has he been trained to cause the maximum of unconsciousness with the minimum of damage? Will his assistant thoughtfully place a cushion under the client's head as they sink to the ground? Will the client's purse, bag or wallet be delivered promptly to their home address minus only the usual Guild fee? We think not!

And then it should be remembered that a high proportion of Guild income finds its way back to the city treasury in the form of taxes, and a prudent citizen who has carefully kept their Guild receipts will receive a modest reduction in their own personal taxes.

Of course, we are aware that a number of people are taking advantage of this and trying do-it-yourself crime, in order to cut out the Guild and save a bit of money. There is no law against this. It is the right of everyone to hit themselves over their own head. But I must say that the Guild is now often being called in to sort out DIY crimes that have gone wrong, and we are forced to make a special charge for this service.

This year we are revising our suite of contracts to offer something for every householder or businessman, whatever their circumstances. All come with a suitable wall badge and personal certificate.

SPECIAL AM$100 PLATINUM BADGE

(subject to status, location and availability)

140

Complete immunity from *all* Guild activities for a full 13 months for a family of up to five people! Our premier service for the busy professional. Comes complete with a handsome gilt badge for the property. People will know you have 'made it' when you become a member of our exclusive Platinum Club.

THE 'FORTUNE' BADGE

A tried and trusted favourite of many citizens. A mere $50 gives a family of five entry to the Guild lottery. This year, odds against a burglary are twelve to one, mugging nineteen to one (outside the Shades) and a list of the other current odds is available upon application. In addition, there are upper limits to the value of goods taken. It may not be you! Comes with a set of steak knives!

THE 'STEADFAST' BADGE

Good value at AM$15. Guild operations will be limited to one break-in or street theft without violence per 18 months. Comes with musical dog ornament.

THE 'FEARNAUGHT' BADGE

A budget bargain at AM$10. Not more than one mugging (not too hard) or one walk-in theft per year. Comes with free First Aid Kit.

And remember – the Guild badge on the wall of a property is a signal to all non-Guild thieves to Keep Away. The City Watch have rules about what they can do to arrested non-Guild thieves. We don't. Ask Herbert 'Shady' Shover, or the Hole In The Head Gang, or Billy 'Two Smoking Boots' Fandooley . . . oh, you can't? Well, there you are.

THE TANTY

A HOME AWAY FROM HOME

Every member of the Guild can look forward to spending some time in prison, under our formal agreement with the city government.

Fair's fair, friends. The city formally accepts a certain amount of organised crime, so for our part we accept a certain amount of organised punishment. As Lord Vetinari has said, what people really dislike is a surprise, be it a burglary or a prison sentence. This way, everyone knows exactly what to expect. What is more, the Watch these days comes down very hard on any Guild member who doesn't follow the rules to the letter, so you might find yourself banged up inadvertently, as it were.

The Tanty, a building whose very mention has chilled the blood of criminals throughout and beyond Ankh-Morpork, was at one time the palace de Tintement ancestral home of the Duc de Tintement. It is a dark, damp edifice with no fresh air, food or water, and so will very likely remind you of home. Everything has to be bought from the warders, including the lice (which must be handed back when you leave).

You will probably spend most of your stretch in the Sallydancy, the huge communal cell, where you will meet friends old and new. It's a tough life, but you will have an opportunity to improve your skills and, in fact, the Guild runs extensive courses there. It is also an appropriate time to catch up on your tattoos. Those with extra cash might like to hire a cell in the Crush Yard, where for little more than the price of a mansion in Park Lane you can enjoy a warm fire, clean sheets and food that has not been spat in.

Do not miss the display of Synchronised Casual Brutality by Warden Sir John 'Hairpin' Shrowber and his team on Thursday nights.

INNOVATIONS

WE WELCOME THE GUILD OF LAGS

That free-thinking inventiveness that is such a feature of the Ankh-Morpork mind has led to the new trade of Professional Prisoner, with its own Guild (technically a branch of our own Thieves' Guild).

A number of organisations in the city have objected to its formation on the grounds that it is morally wrong to pay someone else to take your punishment for you, but Lord Vetinari is reported to have said: 'Ladies and gentlemen, this city has formal organisations of assassins, beggars and thieves… What was your point, exactly?' He also mentioned the speed with which many organisations informally appoint an 'official' scapegoat when caught swindling widows out of their savings and other enterprising activities. The scapegoat takes the blame and the large 'golden boot', while the business continues happily, quite untainted by 'his' sins. At this point, the meeting broke up.

Be that as it may, those of a contemplative disposition, or anxious to make money in a hurry, or who have simply found that life behind bars is preferable (in the words of Joe 'Lifer' Bushyhead, the chairman of the Guild) 'to life in the big prison outside' may find this an attractive career choice. However, Guild rules state that no member must be serving time for more than three clients simultaneously, since beyond that point the combined weight of the manacles is too great.

THE GUILD OF VICTIMS

A new development this year. All members should be aware of it. As far as we can tell, the Guild consists entirely of Mr Echinoid Blacksly, who is offering a service by which he is mugged, burgled or robbed in place of his clients, subsequently sending them a bill. He claims this saves them the inconvenience, bruises, draughts from open windows and so on.

He has petitioned Lord Vetinari on the basis that, if criminals can buy their way out of punishment, victims can buy their way out of victimhood via private enterprise. In an article which appeared in the *Ankh-Morpork Times*, Lord Vetinari is reported as saying that he is minded to approve the application 'because the idea of a man paying another man to spend time in prison for a crime committed against a man in turn paid by someone else to be the victim has a certain classic, nay, poetic symmetry about it. It also provides employment and keeps the money in circulation, which is important.'

We are contesting this, however, since it threatens to make the whole business appear ridiculous.

NEW CRIMES CORNER

144

We in the Guild are always at the forefront of the dawn of the vanguard of the state of the art of the Information Revolution. We like to think that where you find a cutting edge, you will find a member of the Guild threatening people with it.

Therefore the following crimes are being carefully tested for formal adoption by the Guild.

PIGEON TICKLING

Waylaying with big nets the carrier pigeons employed by the less advanced businesses in the city and making use of the information gained. A very promising little crime.

PADDLING

The easy theft of the small portable semaphore systems that are now in use amongst the more stylish members of society.

HACKING

Breaking and entering remote semaphore towers in order to intercept messages and alter the contents of messages for personal gain. This is very highly skilled work and the Company has a policy of Shoot First And Don't Bother To Ask Questions, so pending talks we cannot recommend this to our members.

THE GUILD PROFESSIONS
A SUMMARY

COMMON OR JOBBING BURGLAR

Can we get this one right, lads? We in the Guild do not just shin up a ladder and pinch things. Tradition is what we are about, and it starts with our clothes:

DRESS
Flat cap, domino mask, black and white hooped jersey, black trousers, soft-soled shoes, gloves.

ADDITIONAL
A proper burglar should be badly in need of a shave.

TYPICAL CRY
'You got me bang to rights, guv! Cor, stone the apples and pears!'

EQUIPMENT
Large sack with the word SWAG, jemmy, glass-cutting tool with wad of putty and set of lockpicks.

GENTLEMAN BURGLARS

Too many members seem to reckon that this just means stealing from posh houses during the hours of darkness, but there is a lot more to it than that. A gentleman burglar is supposed to be able to meet his victims socially. We've had a lot of complaints from customers, and quite right too. A lady who is going to lose a valuable diamond necklace is well gutted to find it's being pinched by a man in a hired suit who slurps his soup, puts food in his pockets for later and passes wind happily between courses. They expect flair, they expect excitement, they even expect a little frisson. *Warning*: If you do not know what a frisson is, do not attempt to give one. You will only cause a disturbance.

TYPICAL CRY

'Why, Lady Rust! I haven't seen you since Lady Venturii's End of Season Ball, when the Star of Howandaland was mysteriously stolen from right under our noses!'

{Do not say: *'This asparagus stuff don't half make your pee smell, don't you find, duchess?'*}

DRESS

Starched shirt, white waistcoat, bow tie and evening dress tails. Top hat, with inner pockets for tools. White kid gloves.

EQUIPMENT

Elegant silver lockpicks, glass-cutter, etc. in soft leather roll. Expensive doctor's-style leather bag. Calling cards, usually with a picture illustrating their nom-de-crime. (While it is fine to choose exciting-sounding names such as the Grey Panther or the Silver Fox, it is best to avoid names such as the Pink Red-Bottomed Baboon and the Brown Duck-Billed Platypus. A register of existing names is maintained by the Guild. Please, no more 'Black Shadows'. There are too many already. It's making the Guild sound like a packet of sonkies.)

LADY BURGLARS

A minor but important branch of the art. As with their male counterparts, they are expected to be able to deal with their victims as social equals, although it can become rather complicated and involve knee-to-groin combat. See our special manual. In all cases, a lady burglar should at least be able to escape with what she can carry in her reticule. *Warning*: As with 'frisson', if you do not know what a reticule is, don't guess.

DRESS

Something off-the-shoulder with sequins is generally acceptable. A bustle is useful for those intending to walk out with their swag concealed; failing that, the dresses should be able to be torn easily to allow greater freedom during any chases across the rooftops.

TYPICAL CRY

'La, sir, why don't you pour us a drink while I slip into something more comfortable in that room next door where I saw your emerald cufflinks and the open window . . .' {Don't say: *'I think there's some mistake!'*}

EQUIPMENT

A reticule (very important).

OTHER 'INTRUDERS'

HOUSEBREAKER
Steals from houses in the hours of daylight.

SECOND STOREY MAN
Steals from the upper storey of buildings between the hours of 05.36 and 17.22.

SCAMMLER
Steals from outbuildings.

BOBTILER
Steals from attics, gaining entry through the roof.

MOLECATCHER
Enters buildings via the cellars, breaking through from adjacent cellars.

SOOTYDIVER
Enters buildings via the chimney.

BOMFOOZLER
Enters buildings to steal linen and small china ornaments.

BUGMAN
Enters buildings to steal brooches.

HATTER
Enters buildings to steal hats.

Etc., etc... Friends, there are about 60 different categories of 'people who enter premises to steal things'. This is fair enough. But how much time does it take to check on the notice board before you go out, to see what the other lads in your patch are doing? A dear old lady in Lobbin Clout – and we as a Guild are very respectful of old ladies – has complained that last month sixteen people entered her small house all on the same evening. She tells us that while you were all 'very respectful young men, and quite clean, and one of them was kind enough to lay the fire for me', it was a trial to make tea for everyone. Mr Boggis his own self called on her to apologise and would like it to be known that *anyone* who further inconveniences Mrs Florence Halliwell of 25b Lobbin Clout will 'be put to bed with a shovel'.

BREAKER & DECORATOR

Awonderful addition to the Guild range of activities, since many citizens will pay quite a large premium to avoid the attentions of one of these and even to have them killed. Typically, these are long-haired, extravagantly dressed men who gain entry to their victims' house while they are away (usually on holiday) and then redecorate it in appalling style.

REQUIREMENTS (MALE)

A velvet coat, iron self-confidence and a wonderful way with puce.

REQUIREMENTS (FEMALE)

As above, but possibly also a lot of teeth and a voice you could open a safe with.

151

RAM RAVER

Throws noisy parties in people's houses in their absence, consuming all their food and drink, leaving deposits on their soft furnishings and blocking their privies.

We have been asked to provide this service after very bad reports of the activities of freelance ravers. Under the Guild contract, the selected victims can bargain over the total cost of the exercise and will find their property *carefully* trashed with care and finesse (including the use of Naughty Fido appurtenances where appropriate). At no extra cost, we also arrange for plumbers, decorators, picture restorers, etc., to be on hand immediately after the event.

CONFIDENCE TRICKSTER

Persuades people to part with their money or goods with the false hope of financial gain. They say you can't swindle an honest man, so there is a lot of scope for this job in Ankh-Morpork.

DRESS
Broad-brimmed hat, camel coat, striped suit, spats.

EQUIPMENT
Crafty fag, three cups, three cards.

LACK-OF-CONFIDENCE TRICKSTER

This occupation has become so popular that it is overshadowing the 'parent' occupation. It has enjoyed some amazing success, most notably in the career of Humbert Nussday with his lovely line: 'Oh, Gods, look at me, I'm completely useless, no one's going to buy this bridge off a loser like me, I might as well go and throw myself onto the river right now.' He sold the same bridge three times in one hour.

CLOTHES & EQUIPMENT
Grubby raincoat, hang-dog expression, runny nose.

THEFT ON THE CITY STREETS

ROBBER

Steals (usually in a public place) with the *threat* of force (see Mugger) without being the government.

DRESS

Flat cap, thick-knit pullover, moleskin trousers, big boots.

EQUIPMENT

Club/blackjack, knife.

MUGGER

Steals in a public place with the use of indiscriminate violence. However, a Guild mugger will negotiate points of impact beforehand with the client. *Discriminate* violence is our watchword here. Also remember the Guild ruling that violence is not to be offered to old ladies unless they start it.

153

PICKPOCKET

Steals from the pockets of others, often handkerchiefs. A good introduction to the Guild life for our younger members.

DRESS

Very broad-brimmed, low-crowned black hat, very long, voluminous overcoat full of pockets, soft pointy dancing shoes, fingerless mitts.

IMPORTANT

Just be able to sing, dance and play the flute, in the company of other urchins, strawberry sellers, milkmen and knife grinders, and be so darn cute it makes you sick.

All pickpockets are warned *once again* not to pick the pocket and steal the handkerchief of Cpl Nobby Nobbs of the City Watch. Yes, we know it is easy, but three pickpockets who have achieved it have had to spend weeks in quarantine.

154

PROTECTION RACKETEER

Encourages people to hand over large sums of money in order to protect their property or themselves *without in fact being the government.*

EQUIPMENT

Musical instrument case containing weapon *or* weapon case holding a musical instrument (some people will pay quite a lot of money to get an accordion player off the premises, for example). Coin, for tossing casually while talking to punters.

DRESS

Chalk-stripe suit, loud tie, fedora hat, spats. Do not neglect any of these.

THEFT OUTSIDE THE CITY WALLS

OUTLAW / BANDIT

Broadly the same, except that outlaws have been placed outside the law and bandits have been placed outside the city (literally banished). The most significant difference is in dress, bandits going in for headscarves, gold earrings, etc., while outlaws traditionally wear green and live in the wood.

Neither vocation offers much scope in the city. In fact, the only traditional outlaw in Ankh-Morpork was Wat Snood, while he was hiding from the Chief Forester of Carterhake Forest; the foresters were afraid to follow him and his men when they vanished into the depths of the city, and the outlaws – technically 'inlaws' – were hard to see in their brick-effect jerkins and tights.

The Chief Forester got him in the end by cunningly organising an archery contest and then ordering his men to shoot *on sight* all harmless old beggars seen near the butts (and people carrying long bundles, and anyone with a cart of loose straw). The band were wiped out to a man. It's amazing that such a ruse had until that time never been used by officials who were similarly plagued.

156

PIRATE

Thief who takes property and money on or from the sea or rivers, usually from boats, but possibly from rich fish. Broadly, a damp highwayman without a horse.

DRESS

Very baggy white culotte-style trousers, hooped stockings, baggy boots, sea captain's coat. Hat with skull-and-crossbones motif (skull and crossbones is now the official registered symbol; pirates are no longer allowed to use the skull and lobsters or the skull and kittens).

EQUIPMENT

Cutlass, belaying pin.

OPTIONAL

Firecrackers in the beard, eyepatch, hook (on the end of your *arm*, do not get this wrong).

Still a good career for men and women, with high risks and high rewards.

HIGHWAYMAN

A thief, usually mounted on horseback, who steals from travellers on the open road. But this is a very plain description indeed for one of the most respected of criminal activities, ideal for any man who likes riding in the moonlight and dancing with rather worried ladies, it being a tradition that the highwayman demands a kiss and a dance with the fairest woman in the coach. It is also a good career choice for anyone with a name like Captain Swing, Dr Bones, etc.

However, would-be highwaymen should note that in these cost-conscious days the mail companies are less inclined to enter in the sprit of the thing and it is not unknown for a very heavily armed guard to travel *inside* the coach. Do not ask him for a kiss.

EQUIPMENT

Horse (essential), silver-mounted pistol crossbows, twinkle in the eye (optional), bunch of lace at throat, breeches of doe skin, boots right up to the thigh.

DRESS

Three-cornered hat, caped overcoat, riding boots, domino mask.

THINGS TO SAY

'Stand and deliver! Your money or your life!'

{Do not say: '*I laugh with scorn at your eight-bolt crossbow with the double-strength spri—*'}

157

FOODPAD (OR LOWWAYMAN)

A thief on foot who steals from travellers on the open road. Basically, this is mugging in the nice fresh air.

OTHER SPECIALISMS WITHIN THEFT

BOOTLEGGERS

Those who trade in illicit alcohol, transporting it in containers tucked into their boots.

SLIPPERLEGGERS

Those who trade in illicit alcohol from the comfort of their own home and a large easy chair.

RAM RAIDERS

Groups of youths who purloin sedan chairs (from the Latatian – 'sedere', to sit. Although it may also derive from Sir Sanders Duncombe, the first man to be carried by his servants through the streets of Ankh-Morpork) to break through the windows of expensive stores in Ankh, filling the sedan with booty before making their escape.

JOY RIDERS

Youths who take without consent sedan chairs, rickshaws, bakers' barrows, carts and other wheeled vehicles in order to rush around the streets of Ankh-Morpork at high speed performing stunts for the amusement of their fellows.

COMMON THIEF

The complete all-rounder. A bit of this, a bit of that, a bit of the other (in special cases). Light, opportunistic housebreaking, theft from street barrows, clotheslines, etc., etc. A very popular career.

UNCOMMON THIEF

A new trade. The sky is the limit here. Unicycle, bright red fright wig, clown boots, exploding top hat . . . the important thing is that the victim will be so amazed at the appearance of the thief that they won't know they've been robbed until it is too late. A high-risk, high-reward trade.

159

THE GUILD BUILDING

The casual visitor to Ankh-Morpork can hardly fail to be impressed by the curious façade, or indeed façades, of the Thieves' Guild, sited at one of the most prestigious locations in the city. It occupies the formerly derelict Ankh-Morpork Court House on the corner of the Street of Alchemists and Lower Broad Way, and many have remarked how good it is to see this fine building back once more in the hands of what, broadly speaking, is a part of the legal profession.

The frontage is still very much that of the Court House, a heavily crenellated and portcullis'd façade in Century of the Cheesemite style. The city coat of arms is of course over the entrance, and the dome above, designed by Sir Cranleigh Stamp, is topped by the figure of Justice, holding a bag of gold in one hand and a set of scales in the other (once upon a time, for about the first 12 hours of its existence, the figure was gilded; now it is plated in brass).

Moving up the stone steps past the mock Tsortean pillars, the visitor should take the time to admire the magnificent carved wooden doors, the work of the renowned artist Ralph 'Grumbling' Gibbons. Gibbons, although an exquisite wood carver, was not a happy man and, five days after completing the doors, he killed himself rather messily using a spokeshave.

The marbled entrance hall of the Guild is lit in daylight hours by sunlight filtering through the ornate dome above. The dome's stained glass depicts famous moments in the history of thieving - most notably, of course, the theft of fire from the Gods by the legendary Fingers Mazda, whose statue stands in the centre of the hall.

The statue holds aloft the Undying Flame, which never goes out except on Tuesday afternoons when the janitor tops up the oil.

Ahead of the visitor, beyond the statue, is the magnificent double-curved staircase leading to the galleried upper floors, containing the main hall and the offices of the Guild's principal officers and lecturers. The main hall, three storeys high, has been constructed using wood panelling from the original Ankh-Morpork High Court of Justice. It is used for balls, banquets and examinations. At the end of the main hall is an impressive

dais housing an accurate replica of the Throne of Justice on which, it is said, the Kings of Ankh would sit to hear appeals against the judgements of lesser courts. It is now used when the Guild Council sit in judgement on recalcitrant members, or against unlicensed thieves. A lever to one side of the throne operates the complicated mechanism which causes the throne to slide back into the wall behind it and be replaced by the Guild gallows – its woodwork another riot of rococo carving by Grumbling Gibbons.

Off to one side is the Council Chamber. Note how some of the chairs appear to be fixed to the floor, each of them with what seems to be a closed trapdoor behind it? Note the array of buttons arranged unobtrusively by the chairman's chair? Shortly after its formation the Guild often had to entertain the leaders of gangs who did not wish to affiliate. Shortly after *that*, affiliations climbed quickly.

These, then, with the usual offices, dormitories, storerooms and so on, comprise the main part of the original building. The rear of the premises was entirely rebuilt with the peculiar needs of the Guild in mind.

In pride of place, abutting immediately onto the back of the Court House, is a genuine brick-built Thieves' Kitchen. Tiny-window'd, multi-chimnie'd, its bottle shape almost dwarfs the original building. The Kitchen is now in fact the social and political centre of the Guild, with the Court House building used primarily for official and civic purposes and anything that requires a tilting chair.

162

Within the Kitchen are the Schools of Theft: Burglary, Cutpursing, Pickpocketing, Robbery and Language. Each of these rooms has been designed as an airy and well-equipped lecture hall, with every modern visual aid, including blackboards and . . . well, blackboards is about it, actually. Oh, and chalk. A multi-media room (with coloured chalk, and crayons) is being built.

In addition, there are many rag-hung alcoves wherein all aspects of traditional and modern thievery are taught by visiting lecturers, including Acceptable Cheekiness, Jaunty Repartee and Tap-Dancing (see under Pickpockets). There is also a School of Deportment for Gentleman Thieves and – owing to the Patrician's various decrees that insist that Guild members in most of the disciplines should look the part – an extensive tailoring shop in the basement.

Outside, and effectively constituting the entire rest of the site, are the Practical Science Laboratories – where there are climbing walls with drainpipes and ivy (and with and without protective spikes), mock-up windows in a variety of styles, and doors and skylights to test the skill of even the most accomplished thief. There are also street scenes that include dummy passers-by with booby-trapped pockets, fake stagecoaches, etc., etc. This area is always crowded on the Guild's special Sports Days, where the Long Drop, the 100-yard Scarper, the Nick, Skip and Sidle and, of course, the free-style Nonchalant Walk are all very popular, if unusual, events.

Down some suitably grimy steps are the Guild cellars. Here is the Guild museum, with artefacts from many famous crimes and criminals. The visitor can admire such milestones in the history of theft as the jewel-encrusted jemmy belonging to Claude Tombola who, it is generally accepted, established the genre of Gentlemanly Theft. Here also is the torn, bloodstained tunic once worn by Subaltern Archibald 'Barmy' Postillion, the army officer who stole the Green Eye of the Little Yellow Dog in Klatchistan. The dog itself (stuffed) is also on display.

You will also see, down a further, shorter and narrower flight of stone steps, the dank and uninviting cells used to incarcerate any fortunate individuals whose crimes against the Guild were not so severe as to require the standard death penalty that is the reward for most unlicensed theft. Do not go down that corridor. It is a bad corridor.

Quoted from *The Guild Houses of Ankh-Morpork*, by Startup Nodder, FAMG, AitD (Ankh-Morpork Guild of Architects Press, AM$10)

163

TIPPING THE CRACKSMAN'S CROOK

Giving someone the Guild secret handshake. This is always done with the opposite hand to the one proffered (i.e. if the right hand is proffered, the respondent uses their left). First, the index finger taps the side of the nose twice. Then the hand is extended with the middle two fingers bent back into the palm. The two hands then interlock at right angles to each other, with the joints of the middle two fingers of each hand touching and with the extended fingers touching, respectively, the knuckle of the other middle finger and the crack between the two bent fingers. At the same time, the free hand is formed into the same shape and, being held at shoulder height, is then rocked from side to side for the amusement of the crowd which has, by now, collected.

TALKING THE TALK
A NOSIE FROM THE GUILD RABERCULLY*

Ladies and gentlemen, I'm afraid I once against have to snicker the membership in general for Colleynogging the Talk, or Thieves' Cant. It is depressing or, rather, gritlow. Too many of you vattle just enough mumdoings to pass your exams, and then never scarm with it again. I expect some of you don't even understand what I am voding.

The fact is that thieves have always had their own private language, just as lawyers and policemen do. We must preserve our rich heritage. It is simply no good wearing the right clothes (airing the lob clob) and using the right equipment (bona swiv) if, at the moment of truth, you say 'I'll just open the safe with this lockpick' or 'I'll strike him neatly behind the ear with my cosh'. People will laugh at you. The finger of scorn will be pointed.

Last month one of our members was apprehended by a Professor of Linguistics during a break-in at the man's house in Dolly Sisters, and was summarily knocked to the ground with a thesaurus for failing to understand the term 'scarping the lollymonger'. We could do nothing about it. The professor was quite right to take the view that the man was not a real criminal at all! He was nothing but a moocher, rake-kennel, snap-cove, staler or muppet!

Remember: we are not sneak thieves (except, of course, those of us who are officially Sneak Thieves). Under the terms of the Guild agreement, we must parly treacle-bolly and wagfeather (sound the part as well as look it).

Over the next few months all members of the Guild will have to undertake a written examination to make sure they are properly sevendible and in fine twig, and not mere slumgullet stuff. There will also be spot checks during the work day (or night). Step shokey!1 For those interested, remedial courses will be held in Alcove Three every night for the next month. Remember: If the kins can benshipperly, you're snabbin!2

---

1 *Be warned!*
2 *If the public can understand you, you're doing it wrong!*

PROPOSED CANT TEST, SPECIMEN QUESTIONS

1. You would wear nickerers:

    a) *on your feet*
    b) *your head*
    c) *you wouldn't*

2. If a crib is crusty and it's gimmer, would you:

    a) *use string*
    b) *throw it away*
    c) *sweeve the nodger?*

3. 'Bumpers round and no heel taps!' Is this a good thing? Why?

4. You are holding Queen Bees and Ned Stokes. What are you doing?

5. Translate: 'He twanged the mopsy with a rum morph.'
    Hint: It's a lopgummer mopsy!

6. Guild members are blind siders. Is this statement:

    a) *bonce*
    b) *slumjaw*
    c) *all my eye and betymarsden?*

7. You've Followed the Hen and now you're wearing Captain Hemp's cravat.
    Will your next move be to:

    a) *dance the Tanty hornpipe?*
    b) *do the Washerwoman's Jig?*
    c) *palm the shiv given to you by a confederate and Go On The Lammeroo?*

Explain the reasons for your answer.

165

FINANCIAL SLANG

It is vital to get this right. Saying 'That will cost you five dollars' will mark you down as a very amateur criminal indeed. Names change all the time, but useful terms currently in use are:

DOG	A dollar
GOAT	Five dollars
DONKEY	Ten dollars
STALLION	Twenty dollars
RED-CRESTED WOOD HYRAX	Twenty-five dollars
WHALE	Fifty dollars
MARSUPIAL TOAD	One hundred dollars

Still in use but less common are:

NEWT	Tuppence three farthing
REED WARBLER	Four dollars and two pence
MAGGOT	Twelve dollars thirteen and a half pence
NOB	Fifty pence
HALF A TON	Twenty-five pence
NOBLET	Thirteen pence
COCKROACH	Two dollars twenty-five pence
OYSTER	An oyster

166

ALIBI CORNER

By agreement with the City Watch, the following alibis have been added to the official list. They may be drawn from the Alibi Clerk on a strictly first come, first served basis.

23a   I was in bed but I can't tell you who with

(replaces 22: *'A big guy done it and ran away'*)

66e   I didn't do it because I was committing another crime in another part of the city and already have an alibi for that one

(replaces 66d: *'I was dead drunk that night'*)

141   I didn't do it because I was dining with three bishops at the time

(**NEW**, use with care)

COMPLAINTS PROCEDURE

We must make it clear that complaints against fellow members should be handled by the adjudication committee. We are after all a Guild which uses on a daily basis knives, bludgeons, coshes, shivs, jemmies, acid and big sticks. Someone could get hurt.

We will remind newer members that by arrangement with the Watch an Official Stool Pigeon is appointed each month (see notice board). This is a time-honoured post and he has a job to do. He is *not* therefore to be treated as you might treat an *unofficial* grass. Punishments to be used are:

Tickling the soles of his feet

OR

*Giving him a Klatchian Burn
until it nearly hurts*

OR

Tying his shoelaces together.

The look of the thing is important here.

GUILD OFFICERS

PRESIDENT OF THE GUILD
Josiah Herbert Boggis

STAFF

GENERAL STREET CRIME & SOCIOLOGY
Ben 'Bendy' Fidlam

CONFIDENCE TRICKERY & MODERN LANGUAGES
Mlle 'Madame' Escroc

TEAM-BUILDING & NOCTURNAL CRIMES
Ken 'Nutboy' Cracker

PRISON SURVIVAL & LIBRARIAN
P. 'Screwy' Structor, DCL (Quirm)

EXTRAMURAL CRIMES & HUMANITIES
Horatio 'the Rope Dancer' Räuber

GUILD DOCTOR & FIRST AID INSTRUCTOR
Dr 'Dr Mr MD' Nimgimmer

INTELLECTUAL CRIMES & APPLIED MATHS
Ronnie 'Cheeze It' Boggis

HEAD JANITOR
Jeremiah 'Get off the coke heap!' Cuffin

INTRUSION CRIMES & FENG SHUI
Laurence 'Leeky' Llwyddiannus-Bonheddwr

DINNER LADY
Mrs 'Dreen' Skillagalee

SHOP CRIME & DOMESTIC SCIENCE
Herbert 'Herbert' Glammer

GUILD COUNSELLOR & CHILD PSYCHIATRIST
Mrs 'Mufflin' Dillybag

PROCESS MAPPING & VIOLENT STREET CRIME
Sydney 'Nosher' Lobbygow

SECRETARY
Harry ('Can't Remember His Nickname') Jones

169

WALKING THE WALK

A number of new evening classes (and morning classes for those whose bent requires night work) will be held in the Grass's Gallery for low-grade members and those anxious to brush up their skills.

OCTEDAYS: Menacing, Passive and Active (all Grades)

MONDAYS: Skulking (to Grade Three)

TUESDAYS: Loitering (with Miss Lettuce Babblejack at the pianoforte)

WEDNESDAYS: Shimmying Nodgers (bring own shims)

THURSDAYS: Know Your Hallmarks ('Professor' Albert Snapes)

FRIDAYS: Petty Theft Discussion Group

GUILD TUTORS

JOSIAH HERBERT BOGGIS
President of the Guild

BEN 'BENDY' FIDLAM
General Street Crime & Sociology

KEN 'NUTBOY' CRACKER
Team-Building & Nocturnal Crimes

HORATIO 'THE ROPE DANCER' RÄUBER
Extramural Crimes & Humanities

RONNIE 'CHEEZE IT' BOGGIS
Intellectual Crimes & Applied Maths

**LAURENCE 'LEEKY'
LLWYDDIANNUS-BONHEDDWR**
Intrusion Crimes & Feng Shui

171

HERBERT 'HERBERT' GLAMMER
Shop Crime & Domestic Science

SYDNEY 'NOSHER' LOBBYGOW
Process Mapping & Violent Street
Crime

172

MLLE 'MADAME' ESCROC
Confidence Trickery & Modern
Languages

P. 'SCREWY' STRUCTOR, DCL (QUIRM)
Prison Survival & Librarian

DR 'DR MR MD' NIMGIMMER
Guild Doctor & First Aid Instructor

**JEREMIAH 'GET OFF THE COKE
HEAP!' CUFFIN**
Head Janitor

HEROES OF THEFT

'BLACK JACK' TORPID

Black Jack' is one of the Guild's most celebrated highwaymen, operating predominantly on the Sto Lat road. He is best known as an inveterate ladies' man, who never stole anything more than a kiss from any female passengers on each coach. Recently apprehended by Cpl Nobbs of the Watch, working in plain clothes. Well, not very plain. Taffeta, mostly. With bows.

'JINGLING' JACK GAMMERSTANG

A 7'4" lad from Sto Lat who specialised in stealing chandeliers. Burned alive in broad daylight in Broad Way when all 600 prisms on the chandelier he had just stolen from the Opera House happened to reflect the light in just the wrong way.

REGINALD TRUMPER

Breaking into empty houses to steal the lead off the roof is known, to the criminal fraternity, as 'Bluey Cracking'. Named after Reginald 'Bluey' Trumper, who was the first such thief to successfully sue the house owner for damages when he contracted lead poisoning from eating his packed lunch after removing the lead from their roof.

FATHER THOMAS WHITTLEGATE

Inventor of the speaking tube. Fr Whittlegate used to rob penitents (or, as he put it, remove temptations to sin) while listening to their confessions. He had a speaking tube reaching from his side of the screen along a secret passage to the penitent's rear, allowing him access to their pockets and bags while giving the impression that he was still sitting in front of them on the other side of the screen.

DOBBY STONE

Well-known rogue who specialised in selling worthless amulets and talismen to trusting tourists. One of his favourites - a stone with a hole through it - is now generally called a dobby stone after him. Dobby committed suicide shortly after selling a stone to Salome Tucker, the lady who famously got thirty consecutive winners at the horse races on the same day that she was found to be the lost heiress to the Gazola fortune.

HEROES OF CRIME

'FINGERS' MAZDA

Who first stole fire from the Gods. Technically a demi-god, and currently spending eternity chained to a rock while an eagle pecks out his kidneys. He had been expecting to do community service.

MALE INFANT BOGGIS

Inventor of the dragon-powered thermic lance. He originally intended to burn his way though the walls of the Assassins' Guild strongroom. Contrary to expectations, the work progressed well, and it was only the fact that in a moment of inattention he allowed the dragon to be pointed directly *downwards* that spoiled an otherwise perfect crime. He departed through the ceiling and his charred and frozen remains eventually crashed through a roof six streets away.

JEM MUMLEY

Inventor of the jemmy.

HENRY THE TAUPE

A wizard of Unseen University. While studying criminology, he essayed to see if people could be cheated even after they had been *told* they were being cheated. He set up a Find-The-Lady table in Sator Square and announced to the gathering crowd: 'I *will* cheat so that it will be impossible for you to win! You *cannot* win!' This caused much amusement. Despite the fact that no one won, many customers even returned for another go. Henry made AM\$200 and decided to study human nature instead.

'WEE BILLY' LUDD

A perennially tearful lad whose woeful condition caused kind-hearted passers-by to buy from him 'Chocolate Charlie', a pigeon he claimed to have raised from the egg and which was, he said, his only friend. This transaction is known to have taken place more than 750 times.

SLANG & LINGO

ABSCOTCHALATING FROM THE BUZZ-NAPPER'S KINCHIN A Guild member who's in hiding from a Night Watch officer. Now that the Watch is believed to have recruited a werewolf, an abscotchalater needs to ensure a plentiful supply of strong perfume to cover their own scent.

DARK LANTHORN A dishonest Night Watchman. This was most of them, in the good old days. Beware: any Guild member attempting to bribe a Watchman these days is likely to find his snaphangers caught in a nadgerbog, and no one likes that.

LOBSNEAKING The practice of small boys crawling into shops on their hands and knees in order to get round to the back of the counter to take money from the till before sneaking out the same way. This has to be timed when the assistant is engaged with a customer (who may be the boy's brother or parent). This became so popular in one area of the city that a street became known colloquially as Lobsneaks and has now been officially recognised by that name.

LIGHTING A CANDLE A thief goes into an alehouse to consume a few shants of bivvy (quarts of beer) with the intention of leaving without settling the reckoning (doing a whizzer). In most bars, this is now done only by those members who wish to commit suicide (albeit their suicide is committed for them by someone else).

'HE'S BEEN WORKING UNDER THE ARMPIT'S RECENTLY' 'He's been restricting himself to petty thieving.' Stems from the old days of the monarchy when criminals found guilty of stealing money or goods to the value of more than four groats (e.g., a small wooden box, or a pair of undyed socks, a house in the Shades or a cheese sandwich without pickle) would be clapped by the Watch into an iron halter which they had to wear from arrest to trial. Since this was worn around the neck, those committing small crimes which wouldn't qualify for the halter were said to be operating 'under the armpits'.

DIAMOND GEYSER A senior troll in the Breccia (the troll equivalent of not-very-well-organised crime). Troll criminals traditionally collect the diamond teeth of unsuccessful business rivals, hence the 'diamond'; the 'geyser' part refers to the habit of exploding dangerously when annoyed.

ANGLING Begging from prison by dangling a tin cup on a string out of a barred window. This was a short-lived practice when convicts found they were losing more cups (and string) than they were gaining pennies. Ankh-Morpork, loathe it or leave it!

DUBSMAN A turnkey, or gaoler. Named after a renowned head gaoler at the Tanty - Nathaniel Dubsman, the first head gaoler to have advanced to that position from a start as an inmate of the gaol. Hence the Tanty's other underworld nickname: Dubsman's Hotel.

CHOPPING THE WINERS Lurking around outside temples and churches in order to mingle with the emerging congregation and pick their pockets. Also called 'breaking up of the spell' when done outside the Opera House or theatres, as the audience emerges still entranced by the quality of the performances.

DUMMY DADDLE DODGER A thief who picks pockets under cover of a false hand. Pickpockets have more specialisms than any other branch of theft and these include, for example, 'flimping' (stealing pocket watches), 'fogle hunting' (stealing silk handkerchiefs), and 'aaargh!' (inadvertently picking the pocket of a member of the Guild of Ratcatchers - DO NOT DO THIS).

PANEL GAME A room is wallpapered in such a way as to disguise a softly sliding panel which allows the thief access to a room which the victim thinks is safely locked. This can be a spin-off from breaking and decorating since some skill is required to prepare the crib.

PAVEMENT ARTIST Street dealer in stolen jewellery. Usually they hang around in the jewellery district of Ankh-Morpork; hence their other nickname: Grunefair Pedestrians.

PORCH CLIMBER A second-storey thief.

LUSH WORKING A thief who lies around in grog shops on the dockside, pretending to be a boozington (drunken man), in order to follow drunken sailors with the aim of robbing them. Many a lush worker has discovered that the sailor, too, was only pretending, and has suddenly found himself signed up for seven years before the mast. Worse things happen at sea, as they say, and the boozington will have an unrivalled opportunity to find out what these are.

DOING A MOUSETROUSERS Committing an unprofitable crime. Named after Daniel Mousetrousers, who stole a number of the city's manhole covers in the entirely false belief that they were made of gold. Several of Ankh-Morpork's less observant citizens lost their lives as a result of the Great Drain Robbery, as it became known.

SAWNEY HUNTER One who steals bacon. Someone has to do it.

TILL DIVER One who goes into a shop on the pretence of buying something and then, when the shopkeeper's back is turned, draws out a length of whalebone, daubed at the end with birdlime, and pokes this into the till to draw out the money. It is a shame that this ancient custom has died out in favour of the bludgeon.

RUNNING SMOBBLE Late in the evening, two persons go into a shop, pretending to be drunk. Then, while one of them grabs what he or she can and makes a break for it, the other throws, er, mud into the face of the shopkeeper to distract them from cries of 'Stop thief'.

PREACHING THE PARSON Two men, dressed as Priests of Om, decoy wealthy clergymen into inns or alehouses to drink sweet wines, eat hedgehog-and-vinegar-flavoured snacks and then, by card-sharpery, deprive them of their money or valuables. Seldom used in Ankh-Morpork, where the clergy tend to be rather sharper.

SCUFFLE HUNTING Helping as a porter at the Docks so as to be able to purloin goods and conceal them under the long leather apron worn by such a worker. In some areas, this is also known as 'being a docker'.

SHILLABER The man who, in a con trick, pretends to be a normal passer-by in order to encourage punters into the con with cries like 'My word, this certainly is not a con trick at all, in my opinion!'.

SHOO FLY GAME One man, at an upstairs window overlooking a street, dangles a mock fly on fine thread in front of a punter. Then while the person is distracted dealing with the irritating insect, the fly operator's accomplice picks the punter's pocket. A specialist trick for the sportsman thief.

SLAUGHTER HOUSE A gambling joint which employs people to act as customers who are gambling heavily and winning large sums, in order to encourage punters to part with their money; *also* a gambling house found to be using shaved cards, weighted dice and other tricks. City folk do not take kindly to this sort of thing.

WEARING A SUIT OF MOURNING Having two black eyes.

MUMMING THE MUTTS Using raw meat (occasionally drugged) to pacify guard dogs at storage yards, etc. Traditionally, criminals used to lob a passing dwarf over the fence but, under Lord Vetinari's new rules against discrimination, this practice has largely ceased. Besides, people were losing too many dogs.

SKY LARKER A journeyman bricklayer or builder who gets up early in the morning (with the sky lark) to spot houses with broken tiles, loose mortar, etc., occasionally creating these situations with a well-aimed half brick. He then calls at the house to offer his services and, using the privilege of access given by his trade, 'surveys' the property for his burglar accomplices. The profession has largely died out, since the builder now finds it simpler and more profitable to charge AM$1,700 for fixing the loose tile.

SCRAFFLING To make an escape over rooftops. Named after Bill Scraffle, who disappeared while being chased. He turned up two years later when a bricked-up chimney in Attic Bee Street was re-opened. He had survived by eating pigeons, his own fingernails and drinking rain water, and was fine except for a tendency to scream in the presence of feathers.

PRICKING IN THE TILLYWICKER FOR A DOLPHIN We have not yet managed to find out what this crime is, but apparently it requires a small dog, a length of red string, a chicken and a cardboard box.

THE BLACK SPICE RACKET Holding up chimney sweeps to rob them of their bags of soot. It is not entirely clear why anyone would want to steal bags of soot, but perhaps it is just a niche market. Colloquially used for any theft of apparently worthless items, like old nose hairs, navel fluff and used talcum powder.

SNEEZE LURKER One who throws snuff or pepper in a person's face in order to distract them so that they can rob them with ease. Removing the stuff from the box or jar beforehand is vital.

A GAMMY VENDOR A purveyor of inferior soap who also steals spoons from private houses on Fridays only. A niche profession.

QUOCKERWODGER A wooden image - such as that of a roast chicken - which is attached to a length of string. This is then left on the street and, when a victim goes to pick it up, they are lured into an alleyway where they are belaboured with the wooden image and then robbed. Possibly named after Bernard Quockerwodger, a poulterer in Morpork around 150 years ago, arrested for selling birds whose weight had been exaggerated by stuffing them with wet sawdust. There is no real evidence for this derivation, and Bernard is remembered mostly for what one strong and very angry customer did to him.

RINGING TUGS AND SEATS Going to an event in an old overcoat. The coat is handed over to the cloakroom attendant and a ticket obtained. The thief then peruses the other clientele until he finds one of similar size, surreptitiously swaps cloakroom tickets, and makes off with the victim's smarter and more valuable coat.

FAKING THE DUCK A very dangerous practice. Faking the duck is the watering down of liquor in public houses. Whilst virtually all landlords employ this skill, those who are detected by their clientele frequently find themselves sharing the fate of their liquor, although being chucked into the Ankh does not really count as being 'mixed with water'.

GREAT DAYS IN THIEVING

6 JUNE - FINDER'S DAY

This is the day when the Guild commemorates one of its fundamental principles - Finder's Keepers, Loser's Weepers. On this day, the Guild's principle officers process around the town, picking up any items they 'find' along the route (stray gloves, parked carts and so on; on one occasion, a small building was lifted entirely off its foundations), in order to keep alive this traditional defence against the attentions of the City Watch.

27 AUGUST - BREBB & LEPPIS DAY

A major event in the Thieves' Guild Year, when the entire Council process around the city, visiting each of the gates and proclaiming at each, 'Brebb or Leppis?' This tradition owes its origins to Hugo Brebb and Archibald Leppis, the foolhardy pair who managed to steal a signet ring and monogrammed handkerchief from Lord Snapcase when he was Patrician of Ankh-Morpork, during a State Procession along King's Way on 27 August. Lord Snapcase was so amused by this audacious crime that he commemorated it by having pieces of the two criminals displayed over each of the city's gates for the following three months, with a small competition for school children to see if they could successfully match up all the parts.

12 SEKTOBER - CHASE WHISKERS DAY

Named after Zebediah 'Chase' Whiskers. Whiskers was an expert in the art of robbing messengers and made a lot of money on the side by selling information to the city's ruling classes. Disappeared mysteriously after waylaying a message giving the mysteriously secret location of a mysteriously huge amount of bullion in a house that mysteriously collapsed the moment he went down into the cellar. It is no mystery that the author of the message was Lord Vetinari, who sent a very small wreath to the funeral.

18 EMBER

Tattogey Week. Short Street is given over to street card-gaming and other games of chance normally played in the street. Traditionally, the Watch turn a blind eye to this, as most of the citizens know to avoid Short Street that week and the only real losers are visitors to the city. And who cares about them?

15 MAY

On this day in 1583 Theo Tuckery invented the long flexible cosh and was the first man ever to mug himself.

23 AUGUST

In 1745 burgular Rosie Rosenbloom uttered the famous lines, 'Cor, strike me pink, you got me bang to rights, it's a fair cop, guv'nor and no mistake.' Members are reminded that this is the correct way to behave when apprehended; kicking the officer in the fork and legging it is no longer official Guild policy.

1 GRUNE

In 1801 during this month Chas. Nudder invented the hollow teddy bear, doing wonders for the trade in small items.

23 MARCH

This day in 1911, on a bet among inmates of the Tanty prison, Bistro Frilli ate fifty hard-boiled eggs at one sitting. He lived a further fifteen minutes, but those minutes were full of incident and activity. The chief warder was asked for a report on the incident. He said the report was 'very loud'.

PUSHING THE ENVELOPE WITH
THE POST OFFICE

The novels rarely had the time or space to unfold the 'reality' that Terry and I knew underpinned everything he wrote. When he started to write *Going Postal*, I was delighted to find (through the agency of an online auction house) some ancient Post Office manuals – for the Royal Mail, and also for the US Postal Service. These dusty books were gold mines of material, much of which only needed the tiniest tweak to tone them down for a fictional city.

STEPHEN BRIGGS

When I showed these drawings to Terry for his stamp of approval (ha ha), he particularly liked my depiction of the Quirm Postal Bird. I particularly like my depiction of the dogs with orange eyebrows, because the King Charles spaniel on the right was our own dog, Florence, who used to stare at me whilst I drew, waiting for a biscuit from the 'cupboard of delights'.

PAUL KIDBY

The Ankh-Morpork Central Post Office had a gaunt frontage. It was a building designed for a purpose. It was, therefore, more or less, a big box to employ people in, with two wings at the rear, which enclosed the big stable yard. Some cheap pillars had been sliced in half and stuck on the outside, some niches had been carved for some miscellaneous stone nymphs, some stone urns had been ranged along the parapet, and thus Architecture had been created.

TERRY PRATCHETT

POST
OFFICE

A HISTORY OF THE ANKH-MORPORK POST

In days of yore (about 225 years before olden days, but about 200 years later than ancient times), the Kings of Ankh used messengers to take orders and other messages to all parts of the Sto Plains and far beyond.

The fastest messengers could achieve 200 miles in one day, with frequent changes of horse and cushion at staging, or relay, posts along the route. Riders tended to be young, and on the whole did not grow very old, partly because of the effects on the internal organs of days spent in the saddle of a galloping horse, but also because highwaymen were rife (which is worse than endemic but not quite as bad as ubiquitous). Guards were occasionally sent to flush them out, and there was a gibbet at each relay post to show possible robbers what their likely career prospects were.

And thus the word 'Post' came to be applied to the sending of the mail (the preferred 'Corpse Route' being judged a winner in terms of brand recognition but otherwise lacking in market appeal).

Only the King and certain approved officials, royal relatives, hangers-on and chums were permitted to send letters via the Royal Messenger Service, or Post Boys, but it was not unknown for rich merchants and others to come to private, and highly illegal, arrangement with the couriers.

In those days, the ordinary people of Ankh-Morpork had to rely on the good offices of traders and merchants to carry their mail for them as they journeyed around the Disc. This service was fairly reliable, but letters could take months to arrive, depending on the merchant's destination and the nature of the letter's contents. Merchants, like everyone else, need something entertaining to read of a night by the campfire, and a really good letter might spend years going up and down the trade routes before finally reaching its destination. Daisy's letter to Willie, telling him how much she was looking forward to him coming home from the wars, was on the Ankh-Morpork-Genua route for more than seven years; dozens of copies were made, and it became the subject of a series of postcards and a rather louche cabaret.

188

THE NEXT 'STAGE'

Unseen University set up its own postal service to handle the wizards' personal mail within the city. Owl Post had been tried, but A-M owls turned out to be brighter and less tractable than their rural couterparts, and regarded letters as a warm and easily obtainable nesting material. UU staff did their best to reclaim the post from precarious roosts, and they would eventually be delivered stamped 'Nested on by Owls', although this really did not need pointing out. When an owl has nested for any length of time on your mail, you know it has. You do not need it drawn to your attention.

In AM1530, King Cirone II established a formal network of messengers and horses along important routes, and he appointed a 'Master of the Posts' to administer the system, and to ensure that it worked to maximum efficiency. The first Master of the Posts was Sir Rolande de Colline, who had been a warrior-knight alongside the Assassins' Guild founder, Sir Gyles de Murforte. This high-profile link helped to ensure that the Royal Mail Posts were not subject to attacks by would-be thieves. This system worked quite well, and the term Red Letter Day comes from the fact that the mail was often delivered stained with blood. On the other hand, it had arrived, which was an occasion for rejoicing.

By AM1635, King Lorenzo I (father of Lorenzo the Kind) had decided that the general public could also use the King's Letter Office of Ankh-Morpork and the Sto Plains. The original building, sited on Broad Way, had become commonly known as the Post Office and its chief administrator was now called the Post Master. King Lorenzo dictated at the same time that all houses and properties in Ankh-Morpork should display a number, to facilitate the delivery of the post. There was some initial confusion, when people thought they could choose their own number, and for a while the city was full of Number Ones. In addition, no one wanted to be a Number Eight, that being considered unlucky. This confusion was cleared up in robust fashion when the King sent a squad to pull down every eighth house. Another relic of those days is that every property in Brewer Street is still numbered 34, but this is Traditional and thus considered quaint, not daft.

As the system established itself, all post on the Sto Plains using the Royal Mail had, by Royal Decree, to travel via Ankh-Morpork. This meant that, for example, a letter going from Sto Helit to Sto Lat (a distance of some five miles) would have to journey the twenty miles from Sto Helit into Ankh-Morpork, and a similar distance back again to Sto Lat. The Post Master at the time, Mr Jedediah Palmer, set up a system of new postal routes - called Cross-Posting - which meant mail did not have to travel via Ankh-Mopork. He also introduced the first mail coach service.

Legend has it that the reason for the original Decree has a lot to do with the King's paranoia and the very large black kettle that even now can be found in the Central Post Office.

189

MAIL COACHES

Highway robbery was (and still is) a major problem on the Sto Plains, and the old system of Post Boys left the mail, and its carriers, very vulnerable to attack. The passenger stage coaches fared little better, and travellers rarely arrived at their destinations with all their possessions - or even all their clothes. So Postmaster Palmer set up a system of mail coaches, with a driver and an armed guard on each coach. In the first day of operation, four highwaymen were shot on sight by guards on the mail coaches.[1]

Flushed with success, Palmer tried other tactics, employing for the purpose a number of men with far more scars than teeth, and names like Charlie the Snake. They would travel on the stage disguised as passengers, waiting for an innocent (by comparison) thief to hold it up. A favourite disguise (who can say why?) was 'Governess Taking Three Innocent Young Ladies to Finishing School', but 'Humble Priest' and 'Apparently Drunk And Easy To Rob Elderly Gentleman' also achieved remarkable results . . . so remarkable, in fact, that the populations of entire villages would run away when they heard the coach coming. The new guards did not bother with finicky things like gallows, and generally delivered miscreants to the Post Master in a bucket.

After that, the mail was left alone, and the mail coaches became much more popular with passengers once they heard that 'Governess Taking Three Innocent Young Ladies to Finishing School' would no longer be travelling on that route.

---

1 *That is to say, they were men on horseback and apparently 'looked a bit funny' to the guards. One of them turned out to have documents on him suggesting that he was a travelling seller of patent medicines, but this was taken to be proof that highwaymen are terrible liars.*

POSTAL PASSENGERS

Passengers on the Mail Coach are Permitted to Carry no More than Fourteen Pounds in Weight, at a Cost of One Penny per Pound, plus One Dollar for their own Fare. Such Weight May Not Include Items of a Noxious Nature (Decomposing Bodies, Bananas*, Tuna Sandwiches) nor any Item, any Dimension of Which Exceeds Two Feet Three Inches (2'3").

{*this rule has now been amended to exclude bananas, since the date of the UU Librarian becoming an orang-utan}

POST MARKS

It was during the reign of Lorenzo the Kind that the Master of the Posts, Sir Henry Mark, came up with the system of stampings (which soon became known as 'postmarks') to enable him to time the progress of the mail through the city and beyond - he could then detect inefficient postal stages and slow-moving postal carriers.

Lorenzo the Kind embraced this management tool vigorously and, during the following ten months, the service improved tremendously, although eight tardy Post Boys and seven lazy Sub-Postmasters were hung, drawn and quartered, for the amusement of the citizens and, as Sir Henry said, 'Pour encourager les autres.' Word of mouth - not helped by the King's habit of speaking with his mouth full, plus his courtiers' understandable fear of the consequences of disobedience - transformed this to 'pour encourager les autriches' (ostriches) by the time it had reached Quirm, where the local postal staff immediately started to train these flightless birds to deliver the post in that city. This worked surprisingly well, although the new Post Birds did have a tendency to swallow any amusingly shaped packages. The Quirm Sub-Postmaster met with resistance when he tried to encourage his fellow Sub-Postmasters to use exotic birds as delivery tools. He resented their reactionary attitude and accused them of burying their heads in the sand.

THE DARK AGES

Some hundred years ago, the Post Office began to go into a decline. This was shortly after the construction of the fine new building, conforming to the general rule that all organisations begin to fail the moment they take over a purpose-built headquarters. Success went to the Post Office's collective head. Despite having the most recognised and respected name of any city organisation, it was persuaded by seers and soothsayers to install expensive and untried equipment and change its name to PO!!!!!

People who knew how to do it all were paid to make way for much younger people who didn't know how to do anything at all, and therefore did it badly but much more cheaply. Staff left. The remaining staff worked harder. The new machinery failed to work. Morale fell. The cost of postage went up as efficiency plummeted. Coaches broke down and, as feed and staff bills remained unpaid, the coach drivers took the horses and vehicles in lieu of back pay.

The Post Office stumbled on for decades, but when Ankh-Morpork opened its gates to dwarf immigrants from the mountains, more than doubling the flow of people across the Sto Plains, many citizens took advantage of the dwarfs' informal but reliable couriers. For a while the Post Office maintained a city-wide service, but the End had Come.

HOURS OF BUSINESS

WEEKDAYS

OFFICES IN ANKH-MORPORK

At the larger Post Offices the hours of business are, as a rule, from 8.30 a.m. to 6 p.m., or 6.30 p.m., except on Public Holidays. Exceptionally, some Sub-offices close earlier on Saturdays. All classes of Postal and Clacks business are transacted at the Broad Way Post Office headquarters building between the hours of 8 a.m. and 8 p.m.

OFFICES OUTSIDE ANKH-MORPORK

Larger Post Offices will be open from 9 a.m. until 6 p.m. Smaller local Post Offices may operate shorter hours – 9 a.m. until 5.30 p.m. All excepting Public Holidays. Local small Post Offices may also close early on one day of the week, generally on the local half-holiday.

HOGSWATCH, PATRICIAN'S DAY AND OTHER PUBLIC HOLIDAYS

OFFICES IN ANKH-MORPORK

The Broad Way Post Office will be open from 9.30 a.m. until 12.30 p.m. for all normal services, except for the sales of stamps of a face value of 2 dollars or more and for the acceptance of mail addressed to the Shades, to Borogravia, to Tezuman or to 36 Chitterling Street.

On Hogswatchday, there is one house-to-house delivery of letters and other postal packets within the city walls of Anhk-Morpork (excepting the Shades and 36 Chitterling Street).

OFFICES OUTSIDE ANKH-MORPORK

Local Post Offices may open by local arrangement.

MAIL TO 36 CHITTERLING STREET

Letters to this address will be stored at the Central Post Office until this address reappears in conditions of sufficient stability to allow mail delivery to be attempted.

POSTING BOXES

Members of the public should be aware that new Posting Boxes, now found on many streets, are (a) 6' high, (b) painted red, and (c) furnished with a slot for the ingress of mail.

The Post Office **ACCEPTS NO RESPONSIBILITY** for letters posted into something that is merely 6' high OR red OR possessed of a slot. There have been regrettable incidents.

NOTE 1:
POSTING BOX MAIL EATEN BY SNAILS

We regret that snails are colonising Posting Boxes in the damper parts of the city. Any mail recovered from these boxes may arrive at its destination marked 'Eaten By Snails'.

NOTE 1(a)

The Ankh-Morpork Post Office does not accept that snails eat postage stamps only.

NOTE 1(b)

Following further investigation, the Ankh-Morpork Post Office accepts that snails are particularly attracted to the 50p 'Cabbage Field' stamp. These stamps are being reprinted with a substance in the glue that is harmful to snails but in all probability harmless to humans.

NOTE 1(c)

The Ankh-Morpork Post Office accepts that the new glue on the 50p 'Cabbage Field' stamp leaves an unpleasant aftertaste. Therefore, until further notice, purchases of the 50p 'Cabbage Field' stamp will also receive one (1) Medium Strength Post Office Peppermint free and gratis.

NOTE 1(d)

The Ankh-Morpork Post Office is pleased to announce that the incidence of snails in Posting Boxes should now be severely reduced due to the insertion of official Post Office Toads in all affected Posting Boxes.

NOTE 1(e)

The Ankh-Morpork Post Office accepts that not everyone likes the taste of Peppermint, and therefore every customer entitled to a free Peppermint may opt instead for one (1) violet Jujube.

NOTE 1(f)

The Ankh-Morpork Post Office regrets that measures taken to reduce the incidence of snails in Posting Boxes has resulted in some mail having to be stamped 'Dribbled On By Toads'. To deal with this problem we have taken on a number of Klatchian Melon Snakes.

NOTE 1(g)

Those customers entitled to a Post Office Peppermint or Jujube (see notes 1(c), and 1(e) may in special circumstances be offered one (1) Cherry-flavoured Cough Drop.

NOTE 1(h)

The Ankh-Morpork Post Office regrets that the Klatchain Melon Snake is unfortunately easily confused with the deadly Banded Brown Rumba, even by our suppliers. However, quantities of the anti-venom have now been secured, and staff and customers who feel they might have been bitten should calmly proceed to any Post Office they are reasonably certain of reaching within three minutes.

NOTE 1(i)

The Ankh-Morpork Post Office regrets that it has become necessary to stamp the mail from a few Posting Boxes with the words 'Snake Venom, Deadly on Contact, Open With Care'.

To enable normal service to resume, a number of Posting Boxes are now home to specimens of the Howondaland Red Mongoose, which are totally harmless to humans and cannot possibly be confused with any dangerous breed of creature, even by the most short-sighted and culpable supplier.

NOTE I (j)

The Ankh-Morpork Post Office regrets that it has become necessary to stamp certain items of mail 'Defecated Upon By Mongeese'.

NOTE I (k)

The Ankh-Morpork Post Office has followed with interest the debate in the correspondence columns of *The Times* on the mongooses/mongeese controversy, but takes the view that this is not the point at issue. They still defecate, apparently almost continuously.

NOTE I (l)

The Ankh-Morpork Post Office regrets that it has had to stamp some mail: 'Found Being Used as Bedding By Hamsters', but wishes to point out that staff are almost certain hamsters have not been formally inserted into our Posting Boxes. We believe this is the work of a Prankster.

NOTE I (l) {SUPPLEMENTAL}

The Ankh-Morpork Post Office takes similar views on the occurrence in our Posting Boxes of kittens, lizards, and Mr Edward Souser, 21, of 11 Pellicool Steps, apparently on his stag night.

NOTE I (m)

The Ankh-Morpork Post Office is pleased to announce that it is inviting gnomes and small gargoyles to take up residence in our Posting Boxes, a move which will increase the security of the service and make a valuable contribution to the housing stock of the city.

NOTE I (n)

The Ankh-Morpork Post Office regrets that, following the recent very high tide and flooding in the Rivergate area, it has had occasion to stamp some mail 'Nibbled By Unknown Marine Creatures'.

An official lobster has been acquired.

MISCELLANEOUS REGULATIONS

STAMPS

All letters posted in Ankh-Morpork must carry the postage due for their intended destination in stamps approved by the Postmaster General. No other stamps are acceptable, no matter how pretty they are.

Letters posted in Ankh-Morpork for onwards transmigration by the Semaphore or clacks must carry sufficient postage to cover overland travel at the destination. Tariffs are on display at all Post Offices.

All stamps issued by the Post Office remain valid at their face value for all time, provided that they remain legible. However, this does not apply to the Special Edition 50p Green 'Cabbage Field' stamp, **WHICH MUST NOT BE AFFIXED TO AN ENVELOPE.** This stamp has a gum derived from kohlrabi and cauliflower, intended to give expatriate customers a whiff of home. Regrettably, this has proved to be all too realistic.

It is believed, following the fumigation of the Post Office and four coaches, that the few remaining stamps are in sealed jars, in the hands of private collectors or the City Watch. Anyone in possession of such a stamp **SHOULD NOT TAKE IT TO THE POST OFFICE** but should instead arrange to meet a member of staff in a suitable open space to hand it over in exchange for safe stamps to an equivalent value. **Do Not Lick It Or Allow It To Become Wet In Any Way.**

LETTERS

WEIGHT AND SIZE
There is no limit of weight. The limits of size are:

MAXIMUM:
Two feet (2') in length, eighteen inches (18") in width and eighteen inches (18") in depth; or if made up in a roll, three feet three inches (3' 3") for the length and twice the diameter combined, and two feet six inches (2' 6") for the greatest dimension.

MINIMUM:
Envelopes less than four inches (4") in length by two and three-quarter inches (2¾") in width must not be used.

INADMISSIBLE ARTICLES

Eggs, fish, poultry, game, rabbits, meat, fruit and vegetables are not transmissible by Letter Post and certain articles may be sent only if specially packed (see 'Packing and Make-up' below).

Coupons, forms, cards and so on, bearing written answers to acrostics and guessing competitions, and written communications indicating, whether by means of words, marks, letters or numbers, moves in a game of Thud, are inadmissible.

Stationery, when sent not filled in to a person who is subsequently to use it, is inadmissible. However, not more than three blank forms of a kind, or three of each kind of dissimilar forms, may be included in a packet with a covering document which is itself admissible.

Yearly diaries are admitted, but diaries for shorter periods are inadmissible.

Blotting paper and similar substances are not regarded as ordinarily used for writing or printing and are inadmissible, but a single unfolded flat sheet of blotting paper and not sent as a sample, or one having affixed to it such an advertisement printed on ordinary paper or cardboard, is admitted in suitable open cover.

202

PROHIBITED ARTICLES

Prohibited articles will be refused or detained. These may include:

- Certain circulars
- Fortune-telling Advertisements
- Lottery tickets
- Unsolicited circulars from money lenders

DANGEROUS ARTICLES

Inflammable, noxious, corrosive, deleterious or otherwise harmful articles. Sharp instruments not properly packed. Improperly deactivated magical items of any kind. Matches of all kinds.

Hogswatch crackers are, however, permitted.

Any packet which is likely to pick a fight with or injure either other postal packets in the course of conveyance, or an Officer of the Post Office, or any other person who may deal with that packet.

OTHER PROHIBITED ARTICLES

These would include:

- Contraband

- Counterfeit money or postage stamps (including stamps which, while formally printed for the Post Office, have for any reason been withdrawn, e.g. the 'Lovers' stamp {see p. 218})

- All animals, birds, fish and insects, with the exception of bees, leeches and silkworms

- Indecent[1], obscene or grossly offensive communications, marks, designs, prints, iconographs or other articles, unless they are sent stoutly sealed and have been counter-stamped by the Guild of Seamstresses

EMBARRASSING PACKETS

Packets embarrassing to the Post Office staff are also prohibited. Embarrassment may be caused by the method of addressing and the affixing of the stamp; the colour, type, shape and dimensions of the envelope.

Examples would be:

Addresses mis-spelled so as to give rise to a humorous double entendre.

Stamps positioned adjacent or even above one another in such a way as to cause embarrassment, for example, the superimposition of the common One Penny stamp onto another denomination in such a way that Lord Vetinari appears to be sniffing the backside of a horse.

Any packet wrapped in such a way that it resembles certain private portions of the male human anatomy (specimens are on view to all male callers over the age of 21 and married female callers over the age of 30, by appointment).

203

---

1 *The Post Office is prepared to accept mail such as postcards, which conform to the categories of Naughty and Saucy, but draws the line at Rude.*
Customers wishing to satisfy themselves on this score may, upon payment of a small sum, peruse the representative selection of all categories available on request at the Central Post Office.

OFFENSIVE ACRONYMS AND MISPLACED COSMETICS

By custom and practice the acronyms SWALK, LANCRE and KLATCH are allowed on the reverse side of envelopes containing messages of a romantic nature.

HOWONDALAND, TWOSHIRTS and GENUA, however, are strictly forbidden, unless clearly part of the address. Anyone proposing any other acronym MUST FIRST show it to Miss Maccalariat, Head of Counter Services, who may approve it in the *extremely* unlikely event that no obscene or suggestive meaning can be determined. While 'Sealed With A Loving Kiss' may well be romantic, customers should remember that a letter will share the postbag with many other letters, and both scent and lipstick are notoriously contagious in these circumstances. A letter between senior male business partners that reeks of *Nights of Passion* may cause unintended results. And, of course, lipstick in the wrong place is always difficult to explain away.

PACKING AND MAKE-UP

Letters and postal packets of every kind must be so made up as to not only preserve the contents from loss or damage in the post, but also not to injure any other packets, or any Officer of the Post Office.

Any fragile article must be packed in a container of sufficient strength and surrounded in that container with sufficient soft material or wadding to protect the article from the effects of concussion, pressure and knocks to which postal packets are ordinarily exposed. The packet must bear the words FRAGILE WITH CARE written conspicuously on the face of the cover above the address, so that Postal Officers will know which packages will need to be tested to ensure that they can withstand dropping from great heights, stamping on, kicking, hitting with lump hammers, and any other normal treatment that would be given to such a package.

EGGS

These are a challenge to the Postal Worker, and their safe transit cannot be guaranteed. If you want to risk it, you might try using a wooden box with suitable partitions and a well-fitting lid, wrapping each egg separately in newspaper or other soft material, placing the eggs on end, each in a separate partition, and filling up the vacant spaces in the box with newspaper or cotton waste. The parcel should be marked EGGS so that time is not wasted testing a parcel containing, say, rock samples.

BUTTER, CREAM AND OTHER SEMI-LIQUIDS

These and greasy or strong-smelling substances must be so packed that they will not soil or taint other packets. For example, a tightly lidded tin, secured with sealed string crossing the lid in two directions, then wrapped securely in greaseproof paper and placed in a well-constructed wooden box.

FISH AND OTHER MEAT

(Not including body parts travelling by mail between Igors; see next page). These should be sewn into rush baskets, straw matting, sacking, or similar material, with sufficient internal waterproof wrapping or absorbent packing to prevent the contents from damaging or tainting the outer covering and thus making the parcels objectionable to handle for human Officers of the Post Office.

LIQUIDS

These may be sent in tins or bottles (securely sealed). Containers of a pint or more must be contained within a wooden box or wicker case, making good use of soft packaging to prevent damage in transit. Wow-Wow Sauce certified as less than five days old at the time of posting will be carried outside the coach at the discretion of the coachman, and only if the journey is expected to be not very bumpy. Wow-Wow Sauce aged five days and over is not allowed on Post Office premises or in Post Office vehicles.

OTHER SERVICES

IGOR 2 IGOR

Members of the Igor clan are invited to avail themselves of this Premium Service. The weekly Ankh-Morpork to Genua run, via Uberwald, can by arrangement take iceboxes big enough for most human organs in a capacious and very well insulated compartment. For those requiring a full, dedicated crypt-to-crypt service, call at the Central Post Office for our pamphlet 'Igor2Igor: Foreign Parts Are Closer Than You Think!'[1]

---

1 *Persons using the Igor2Igor service must ensure that the organs are in a strong icebox and, whenever possible, in a quiessant and non-aggressive state. This particularly applies to hands.*

SOIL OF THE HOMELAND BEING SHIPPED TO OR POSSIBLY CONTAINING CERTAIN CITIZENS OF UBERWALD

To be accepted in the Post, this must be enclosed in a secure wooden box, screwed down at no fewer than twelve-inch intervals and transported in such a way that it will be in transit only during the normal hours of daylight. Under no circumstances will such crates be accepted for transit by ship. Such crates must clearly be marked NOT TO BE HANDLED DURING THE HOURS OF DARKNESS.[1,2]

---

1 *Mail coaches travelling to or through Uberwald must carry Travelling Kit 3 (supplemental), comprising: one (1) flask Ecumenically Holy Water; two (2) stakes, wooden; one (1) hammer.*
2 *The Soil of the Homeland Regulation applies only to those holding a valid membership of the Uberwald League of Temperance. Others attempting unfairly to obtain cheap travel by this means should be aware that the standard carrying box is fully airtight and is not opened en route, no matter how much hammering there is on the lid.*

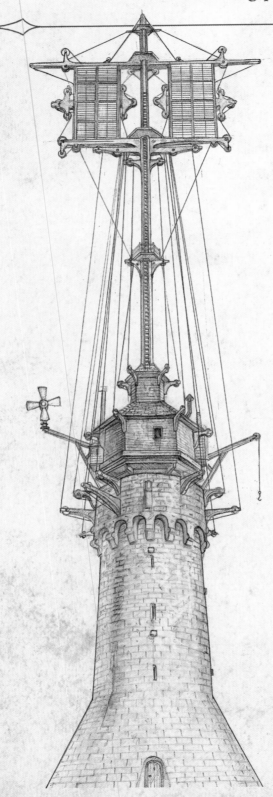

208

'AIR POST'

The Post Office is pleased to announce a new service, to make the Grand Trunk Semaphore System more accessible by those uneasy with new technology.

Yes, letters that once would be carried by coach can now arrive in a matter of hours at destinations as far away as Uberwald!

The De Luxe Service is door-to-door. The letter will be collected by one of our nimble Semaphore Lads (the 'Speedies'), carried smartly through the most crowded of streets to the nearest semaphore tower, 'en-coded' and 'transmigrated' thence to the distant tower closest to the eventual destination, whence it is 'de-coded' and then delivered by messenger.

A tariff is available at most towers and all Post Offices.

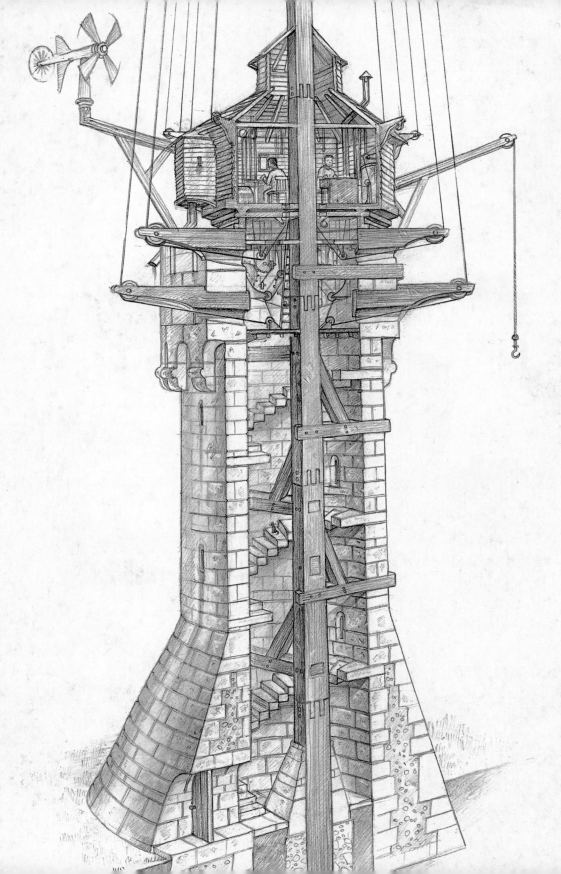

MOBILE POST OFFICES

These may be set up from time to time at major events for the sale of stamps, the franking of special covers, the sale of stamps, miscellaneous Post Office Services and, of course, the sale of stamps. Staff manning Mobile Post Offices will on demand produce their accreditation from the Postmaster General.

A small Mobile Post Office has been set up in Koom Valley for those citizens working or posted there during the current Truce and Negotiations. By Decree of Lord Vetinari, letters affixed with the new Koom Valley stamp will be delivered there at normal internal city rates.

MAGIC ITEMS CARRIED BY THE POST

The Post Office has special rates for magical items carried in the mail.

Wizards' staffs will only be transported if accompanied by their owner.

Deactivated cauldrons, sealed potions, wands and pointy hats travel at normal parcel rates, as do (deactivated) broomsticks.

Activated broomsticks maintaining full lifting power will be carried free.

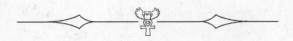

211

GREAT DATES IN POSTING

4 OCTOBER 1530

Sir Rolande de Colline appointed as the first Ankh-Morpork Master of the Posts, with a salary of three shillings a month, plus two rabbits, a pound of turnips and a flagon and a half of ale.

1 APRIL 1635

Master Lambert Cordwainer becomes the first commoner customer of the new postal service. Master Cordwainer sent a letter to himself at his home address in order to 'teste thee system'. Cordwainer's original and unopened letter was recently sold on C-Bay for AM$ 150,000.

30 SEKTOBER 1635

Installation of the first official Post Office Cat. Known as 'Mr Tiddles', the cat remained in office for an amazing twenty-three years, during which time the CatLog shows he killed 1,137 rats, 1,563 mice and voles, 212 small birds, and one junior Post Man (the cat dislodged a piece of loose masonry which fell on the unfortunate Mr Trinder).

27 AUGUST 1650

Nine forty-five a.m. First letter delivered to Genua from Ankh-Morpork by the King's Letter Office, having been handed in to the office on Broad Way at twelve minutes past three on the afternoon of 23 August 1649.

25 GRUNE 1722

Master Richard Scallion is the youngest person ever to be dismissed from the Postal Service, for writing 'Oh Yes They Do' on a package for the Duke of Eorle bearing the inscription 'PRICELESS ENGRAVINGS - DO NOT BEND'.

16 APRIL 1732

Installation of the statue of the winged God in the central concourse of the Ankh-Morpork Post Office. The statue is the work of the great sculptor Auguste Buonarotti, who also carved the cherubs and other gilded figures decorating the Opera House. The winged God is believed to have been based upon the sculptor himself, although this was disputed at the time by Signora Buonarotti.

27 DECEMBER 1762

Publication of the First Edition of the Post Office Regulations. Previously, these had been handed down by a combination of oral tradition and a large box-file stuffed with Royal Commands and letters from Head Office.

24 JULY 1797

The Post Office welcomes its One Millionth Customer, Mrs Sylvestra Wincot. She is presented with a dozen pre-stamped envelopes, an engraving of the then Post Master (Mr N. Aushilfe) and a souvenir bottle of blue-black ink.

31 MAY 1798

The rules for the operation of Sub-post Offices were relaxed to permit the sale, on the premises, of a range of grocery produce but also including stationery items, hair grips, sink plugs, hair combs and novelty false nose/moustache sets.

213

214

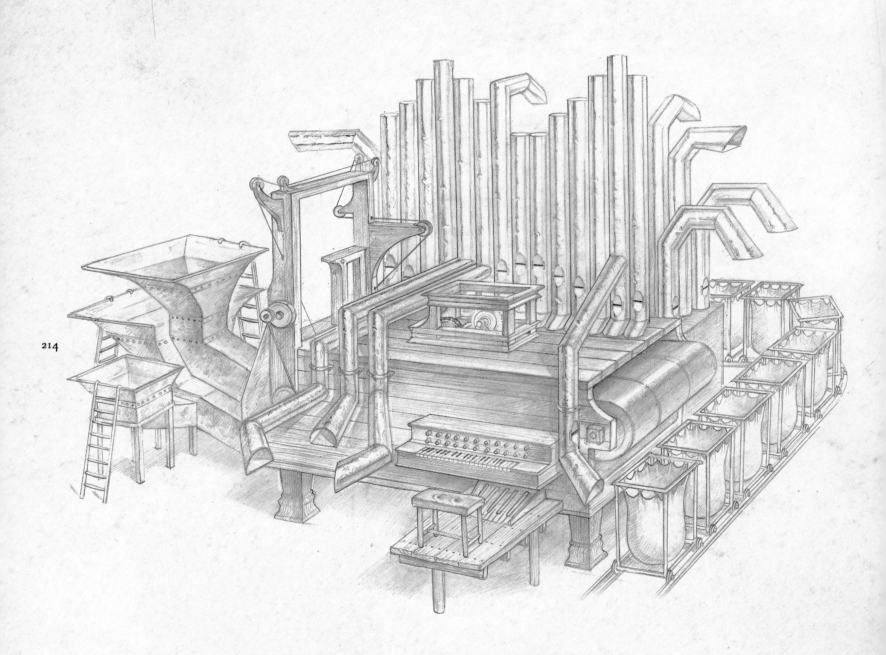

THE SORTING MACHINE

18 JULY 1798

Publication of the Fourteenth Edition of the Post Office Regulations. Known to bibliophiles as the 'Tiny Post Book' because of a typographical error on page 127, so that the rules stated: 'Envelopes less than four inches (4") in length by two and three-quarter inches (2¾") in width must be used.' The omission of the word 'not' led to the Broad Way Post Office being presented with more than two thousand letters measuring around one inch (1") by half an inch (1/2") before the edition could be recalled and corrected.

3 JANUARY 1805

The Post Office motto is installed on the front of the building. The motto was agreed upon following a competition amongst postal workers, narrowly beating its close rival 'WE'LL DELIVER IT IF WE FEEL LIKE IT AND NOT BEFORE'.

13 FEBRUARY 1815

The Post Master, Sir William Guilfoyle, introduces a pneumatic tube system to deliver money and change between the Cashier's Office and the front counters. Sadly, this had been designed by BS Johnson and, after a number of holes had been punched into the fabric of the building by supersonic tubes of small change, he was encouraged by the Patrician to suspend the system.

12 DECEMBER 1876

Delivery of the first stocks of rubber finger stalls, following the death of a Counter Clerk who had licked his fingers to turn the pages of a book being delivered to a local Monastery.

13 JANUARY 1877

Mr William Sonkey personally replaces the delivery with the correct rubber product following complaints from female Counter staff.

21 NOVEMBER 1878

First performance of the Disc's first Postal Opera, 'Die Postmeistersinger von Uberwald'. This was a massive success and played to packed houses until it was ousted in popular appeal some two years later by the even more popular 'Das Zaubebriefmarkenalbum'.

1 MARCH 1888

The Great Post Office Almost Robbery. Masked men, armed with pistol crossbows, entered the Mail Room at 02.45 a.m. on the first of March. They overpowered the duty Post Man but, in their haste to pack as much Registered Mail as possible into their waiting cart, it seems that they fell into the Sorting Machine. They were subsequently arrested by Captain Vimes of the City Watch on 2 March 1983.

1 OCTOBER 1900

Tailcoats cease to be a part of the Postal uniform when the first female Postal Delivery Operatives are employed. The only exception is the frock-coat still worn on ceremonial occasions by the Post Masters.

16 MAY 1978

The first 'Mail Order' service is set up by Mr CMOT Dibbler, a tradesperson of Ankh-Morpork. Despite the name, Mr Dibbler's service also extended to sheet armour.

17 MAY 1978

The first 'Mail Order' service is closed down by Lord Vetinari, who does not approve of the use of 'punes' or plays on words in the mission statements of city businesses.

STAMPS OF NOTE

TWOSHIRTS 2p CABBAGE FESTIVAL STAMP

Celebrates the Cabbage Macerating Festival in Twoshirts. This stamp features a picture of two gentlemen treading cabbages in a large vat.

THE PENNY PATRICIAN

The first stamp produced by Messrs Teemer & Spools. It shows a fine burlage to the background over which is an engraved portrait of the Patrician. There is reputed to be a variation where the engraved plate was somehow damaged on part of the central image. This gave the appearance of some grey hair on the head of the Patrician. Once noticed, this particular issue was withdrawn and destroyed; however, a few stamps might be in the hands of some very careful and discreet collectors.

BAD BLINTZ STAMPS

The town of Bad Blintz, a great tourist centre and famed as the town that made a pact with a clan of intelligent rats, has issued stamps in the following values: 1 blzot (Brown, showing a smiling rat); 2 blzot (Red, a view of the Rathaus); 5 blzot (Blue, The Rat Piper); 10 blzot (Black, The Ratcatcher Museum); 20 blzot (Green, The Rat Clock); 50 blzot (four-colour, The Dancing Rats); and the 100 blzot (four-colour, showing a representation of Wotua Gram's famous painting *The Signing Of The Pact*). In the interests of equality among all its citizens, Bad Blintz has also issued miniature stamps for the use of the rat population, which are of great interest to the collector.

TOWER OF ART

Depicting the Unseen University Tower of Art amid its scholastic environment. A most unusual stamp with reports of transfiguration within the engraving. The first transfiguration is where the bird to the right of the tower is replaced by a man in free fall. The second inexplicable transfiguration is a small splash visible in the water near the base of the tower.

THE ASSASSINS' GUILD THREE PENCE STAMP

This was issued after problems with the gum on the Assassins' Post-Paid. This letter stamp, known as the Zombie Stamp, or Thrup'ny Dreadful, was withdrawn after unsubstantiated rumours that the Guild was using its stamps to poison 'clients'. After the outcry and possibly coincidental funeral, the remaining Post-Paid stamps were withdrawn. A few stamps have found their way onto the market and are of interest to collectors. A sealed transparent envelope is advised.

217

RAT STAMPS

Rats have only a limited use for currency, but extremely small gold, silver and bronze coins have been minted and are known respectively as the Candle, the Medium Potato and the Raisin. Rat stamps to the same values are printed and paw-perforated by the rats themselves. All three are coloured red, brown and black, and show the relevant object and the phrase 'Rattus Sapiens' in human and rat scripts. They are on sale in Bad Blintz Post Office. The Raisin, the Medium Potato and Candle stamps are equivalent to the Bad Blintz 'human' 1, 5 and 20 blzot stamps.

THE 50p GREEN 2nd ISSUE STAMP (THE SO-CALLED 'LOVERS' STAMP):

AN OFFICIAL STATEMENT

There has been much scandalous talk about this stamp, which is now withdrawn. THE FACTS are as follows:

The Post Office commissioned a new painting for the 2nd Issue of this popular stamp, this time showing, at the suggestion of the Cabbage Growers' Association, a field of Micklegreen's Juicy, an improved variety, rather than that old stalwart, Autumn Reliant.

It just so happened that while our artist was working, a young man chose to use that field for the purpose of teaching a young lady to hoe. The arts of hoeing are of course much prized among the growers of the Plains, and a young woman who can turn her hand to the hoe, it is said, will never want for a husband.

It transpires that, whilst essaying a particularly tricky root aeration manoeuvre, the young woman noticed our artist and, overcome with maidenly modesty, mishandled the implement and caused both herself and her tutor to collapse among the brassicas, in, obviously, some considerable disarray, and not to say déshabillé.

For his part, our artist, being city-born, was not to know that this was not just another agricultural procedure, and continued sketching in the belief that this would add 'colour' to the finished stamp. In this he was, we regret to say, prescient.

It was only after several hundred sheets of this stamp had been printed that it was put to our Officer in Charge of Stamps, Mr Stanley Howler, that those of a perverse and mischievous disposition might put a different, and we have to say, entirely unwarranted interpretation on the depiction. We are *assured* by more senior members of the Association that the young man was most probably demonstrating the fine old rural practice of 'shuggling', which is the warming of the seed-bed with the buttocks before sowing. It is good to see the old Traditions being passed on, and unfortunate that some people have used the Press to traduce them with questionable and not at all funny remarks.

Regrettably, a very few of the early run of the stamps also showed Lord Vetinari's head tilted slightly, as if he had decided to take an interest in bygone agricultural practices.

Because of the unwarranted assumptions made, this stamp was withdrawn and is not valid for use on letters. We are aware that a number of sheets have found their way into general circulation. If presented at a Post Office, they will be exchanged for stamps of the same value.

This unfortunate episode is closed.

Nice try, Tolliver. I almost believe it myself. Do have that 'special' talk with young Stanley, will you?
By the way, they're fetching $50 each at Dave's Stamp & Pin Exchange. Have we got any more?

Lipwig

219

HEROES OF
THE POST OFFICE

POSTMASTER NORBERT ANDERS

Norbert Anders was the man who came up with the slogan 'Post Early for Hogswatch'. He also came up with 'Always Use the Post Code', although it was to be more than 140 years before anyone knew what that one meant.

TEMPORARY HOGSWATCH POSTMAN RODNEY POSTLETHWAITE

Rescued his mentor, Snr Postman Jess 'Jessica' Thrupp, from a nasty mauling by two of Harry King's Libwigzer dogs by belabouring the animals about the head with a frozen leg of lamb he had been delivering to the shop next door. He received the Post Man's Medal of Valour.

COUNTER CLERK MISS ALEXANDRA WILLETT

Devised the system by which customers needed to queue separately to purchase stamps, send a parcel and renew a cart licence. This meant jobs for three staff when previously only one was needed, and it greatly increased the confusion of merged lines of customers in major Post Offices.

SIR ARTHUR BRADY

There is a plaque to the memory of Sir Arthur Brady, the Morporkian composer who, in 1649, wrote the Post Horn tunes which have been used ever since by the mail coachmen. These include 'Express Mail Coming Through', 'Runaway Horses' and 'Make Sure There's a Clear Path to the Privy When We Draw Up'. Sir Arthur's only other well-known tune is the backing to the famous Omnian hymn 'Om is Crushing the Infidel with Large Rocks'.

POSTMAN HENRY SLOOP

The only Post Man on record to have delivered two hundred and forty-seven 'Sorry you were out' cards without ever once managing to deliver the parcel.

POSTMASTER GENERAL ELWES

Elwes is credited with being the man who introduced the queuing system into the Ankh-Morpork Post Office. In the 25 years prior to that innovation, twelve people had died fighting to send a postal packet and one person lost the use of a leg in an effort to hand in a delayed tax return.

JUNIOR POSTMAN HAROLD POOTAH

In 1737, Junior Postman Harold Pootah found, at the bottom of his mail sack, an envelope addressed to a Master James Shovel of 32b, Shamlegger Street. On arrival at this address, Mr Pootah found that the Shovel family had moved the day before to Genua. Not to be beaten, Jnr Pstmn Pootah set off, on foot, and – two and a half years later – delivered the letter to Master Shovel. When he got back to Ankh-Morpork, he was dismissed for being absent without leave. Three months later, a thank-you letter arrived from the Shovels but by then Harold Pootah had hanged himself – too ashamed to live on. He is the Post Office's only martyr. To date.

JEDEDIAH BERK

Jedediah Berk, of the Guild of Alchemists, became the unsung hero of generations of Post Mistresses and Counter Clerks in the Package Repair Office when he invented the rubber roller in a small trough of green, smelly water – a device which liberated them from having to lick miles of brown sticky tape each Hogswatch, mending badly constructed parcels. The glue on the government-issued tape is a compound of boiled slugs and horse bones.

ROBERT HUMMINGBIRD

Robert Hummingbird, a clerk in the Central Ankh-Morpork Post Office, was the person who thought of filling the handle of the 'FRAGILE' stamp with lead shot, to give it greater ability to make an impression.

SNR POSTMAN GRANVILLE ROBERTS

On 15 Sektober 1841, Snr Postman Granville Roberts was delivering a parcel to Sir Despard Pontefract at his home in Scoone Avenue, when one of Sir Despard's hounds, Saliva, ran into him, causing him to lose his grip on the package, which was marked 'Extremely Fragile'. Roberts threw himself full length to the floor to catch the parcel (containing, as we now know, an almost priceless cut-crystal decanter attributed to Vermicelli). In doing so, he landed on the dog, Saliva, who sank his fangs into Postman Roberts' leg. Despite the pain, Roberts saved the parcel and dragged the dog (still attached to his leg) up the 200-yard drive to the front door, where he handed the package to the Pontefracts' butler before collapsing from loss of blood.

COUNTER CLERK MISS AMELIE WILLETT

Miss Willett introduced the idea that Post Office forms should be revised on a daily basis, to ensure that once a customer reached the counter, they would almost certainly have the wrong form and would have to go back to the end of the queue.

MISS HONORIA MACCALARIAT

Miss Honoria (an ancestor of our current Post Office colleague) saved the Post Office thousands of dollars when she suggested that the pens should be chained to the counter.

EMPLOYEES

TOLLIVER GROAT

GEORGE AGGY

JIMMY TROPES

SENIOR POST MAN BATES

ASSOCIATES

THE UPRIGHT BROS.

MR SPOOLS

ADORA BELLE DEARHEART

MR PONY

ENEMIES OF THE POST OFFICE

REACHER GILT

CRISPIN HORSEFRY

MRS CAKE

MR GRYLE

224

GOLEMS

MR PUMP

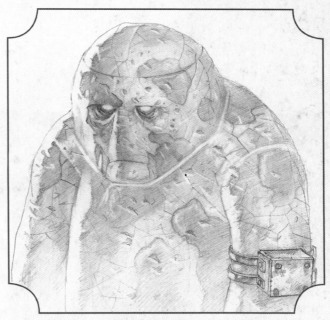

EXTREMELY SENIOR POST MAN
ANGHAMMARAD

Moist knew something about golems. They used to be baked out of clay,
thousands of years ago, and brought to life by some kind of scroll put inside
their heads, and they never wore out and they worked, all the time. You saw
them pushing brooms, or doing heavy work in timber yards and foundries.
Most of them you never saw at all. They made the hidden wheels go round,
down in the dark. And that was more or less the limit of his interest in them.
They were, almost by definition, honest.

Going Postal

GLADYS

Moist turned back to Miss Maccalariat. "Would 'Gladys' do, Miss Maccalariat?"

"'Gladys' will be sufficient, Mr. Lipwig," said Miss Maccalariat, more than a hint of triumph in her voice. "She must be properly clothed, of course."

"Clothed?" said Moist weakly. "But a golem isn't–it doesn't–they don't have..." He quailed under the glare, and gave up. "Yes, Miss Maccalariat. Something gingham, I think, Mr. Pump?"

Going Postal

226

NEW RECRUIT

"And now all that remains"–
he nodded to Stanley, who
held up two bit tins of royal
blue paint–"is their uniform."
{...}

The afternoon sunlight
glinted off royal blue and
Stanley, gods bless him,
had found a small pot of
gold paint, too. Frankly, the
golems were impressive.
They gleamed.

Going Postal

227

NEVER TRUST A DOG WITH ORANGE EYEBROWS

NOTABLE DATES

ICK

1
HOGSWATCH DAY

OFFLE

11
RINGING OF THE BELLS

Annually on this day hooded men patrol the centre of the city at 3 a.m., stopping at the site of the old city gates and ringing the bells. Efforts to catch and prosecute them have failed. (*From the Ankh-Morpork Almanac*)

12
TUMPERS
(*Assassins' Guild*)

FEBRUARY

1
BEATING THE BOUNDS
(*Unseen University*)

(Plunkers) marking the old UU boundaries. Passers-by may be struck with live ferrets, because it is Traditional.

8
EEL PIE AND MASH RIOTS

On this day in AM1823, the famous Eel Pie and Mash Riots took place in Rumpty Street, Ankh-Morpork. Seven people were killed, one by a carelessly thrown eel and six more in civic attempts to restore order. (*From the Ankh-Morpork Almanac*)

22
HOBSTOP & WRIGGLE-MY-SNAPE
(*Assassins' Guild*)

Hobstop and Wriggle-my-Snape may be played on this day, in the long corridor adjoining the Clamp. The winner is, by tradition, awarded a cauliflower.

MARCH

FIRST THURSDAY IN MARCH
OPPORTUNITY DAY
(*Assassins' Guild*)

GAUDY NIGHT
(*Assassins' Guild*)

3
SCRAWN MONEY
(*Unseen University*)

Scrawn Money is paid on this day. Tenants on UU property are given two pennies, a pair of long socks and a loaf of bread because of Tradition.

SECOND SATURDAY IN MARCH
SMAEDI NUITE MORTE
(*Genua*)

Last night of the Mardi Gras celebrations, when the dead can join in. Get down and bogeyman!

FOUR DAYS LATER
LAST NIGHT OF MARDIS GRAS
(*Genua*)

29
RAIN OF SHARKS & JELLYFISH

On this day in AM1447, a freak rain of sharks and jellyfish injured several people. (*From the Ankh-Morpork-Almanac*)

APRIL

1
TURNABOUT DAY
(*Assassins' Guild*)

10
POOR SCHOLARS DAY

The student body is pelted by the faculty with stale rolls, possibly because of Tradition, but perhaps just because they want to.

28
CREATION DAY

MAY

1
MAY MORNING CHOIR SINGS
(*Unseen University*)

Choir sings from the top of the Tower of Art. No one can hear them, but everyone applauds.

MAY BLOSSOM DAY
(*Assassins' Guild*)

25
LILAC DAY

JUNE

4
CONVIVIUM DEGREE CEREMONY
(*Unseen University*)

Convivium Degree Ceremony, now held in the Opera House and always finishing in time for lunch.

7
FINDER'S DAY
(*Thieves' Guild*)

9
MAXIMUM MARKS
(*Assassins' Guild*)

On this day in 1901 William Venturi, then Head Boy, became the first person to complete the new Assassin Test by assassinating the tester. This earned him maximum marks, but the test procedure was thereafter revised.

18
SMALL GODS EVE

19
SMALL GODS DAY/NIGHT

24
TREACLE PIE DAY

Treacle Pie day is still occasionally celebrated by the baking of treacle pies and the burning in effigy of Laughing Lord Scapula, who imposed the rigorous tax on washing lines.

LAST SATURDAY IN JUNE
WIZARDS EXCUSE ME
(Unseen University)

END OF BACKSPINDLE TERM
(Unseen University)

DANCE AND KNIFE & FORK TEA
(Unseen University)

30
FIELD DAY
(Assassins' Guild)

GRUNE

6
PATRICIAN'S DAY

19
INVENTION OF THE PENCIL
On this day in AM1789, Osric Pencillium succeeded in domestically cultivating the graphite-cored, thin-branched bush which now bears his name. Early 'pencils' were very soft 4B varieties.

20
GAUDY NIGHT
(Unseen University)
Wear something tasteless to the grand banquet in the Main Hall.

22
ÜBERWALD LEAGUE OF TEMPERANCE DAY

28
d'MURFORTE DAY
(Assassins' Guild)

A WEEKEND IN LATE GRUNE
GUILD SPORTS DAY
(Assassins' Guild)

LAST THURSDAY IN GRUNE
HEAD OF RIVER RUNNING RACE
Running race with boats on the Ankh.

LAST SUNDAY IN GRUNE
MIZZLING SUNDAY
(Assassins' Guild)

AUGUST

27
FOUNDERS DAY
(Assassins' Guild)

LAST OCTEDAY IN AUGUST
BREBB & LEPPIS DAY
(Assassins' Guild)

SPUNE

3
WITCH TRIALS

USUALLY THE FIRST FULL WEEK IN SPUNE, UNLESS IT CLASHES WITH SOMETHING ELSE IN THE ARCHCHANCELLOR'S DIARY
RAG WEEK
(Unseen University)

LAST SATURDAY IN SPUNE
'SITY AND GUILDS FOOTBALL
(Unseen University)

SEKTOBER

4
CHEESE OUTBREAK
On this date in AM1890, a dozen people were injured in Quirm owing to an outbreak of cheese. *(From the Ankh Morpork Almanac)*

10
PULLIS COVORUM
(Assassins' Guild)

12
CHASE WHISKERS DAY
(Thieves' Guild)

FIRST TUESDAY, WEDNESDAY & THURSDAY AFTER THE FIRST HALF MOON IN SEKTOBER
SOUL CAKE DAY
The Soul Cake Duck brings choccy eggs for good children whose parents can afford choccy eggs.

10
PULLIS CONVORUM
(Assassins' Guild)

17
B.E. DAY

MID SEKTOBER
STO PLAINS TIDDLY WINK FINALS

19
GENERAL INSPECTION
(Assassins' Guild)

25
BALD OCTEDAY

EMBER

15
SLIBBERING BAN
(Assassins' Guild)
On this day in AM1832 the practice of slibbering was forbidden in the school.

LAST FULL WEEK IN EMBER
TATTOGEY WEEK
(Thieves' Guild)

29

DECEMBER

CLOSEST FRIDAY TO THE MIDDLE OF DECEMBER
CAROL SERVICE FOR HOGSWATCH
(Assassins' Guild)

25
BOY ARCHCHANCELLOR ELECTED
(Unseen University)

30
HOGSWATCH EVE
HIRING FAIR
(Sheepridge)
Sometimes attended by very odd characters.

31
HOGSWATCH NIGHT
A season of good cheer and inventive pork products. Leave out a pork pie and a glass of sherry.

Paul sees things my way about seventy-five percent of the time, which suggests either mind-reading is happening or that my vision of the characters is really rather vague until I see his drawings.

TERRY PRATCHETT

ARTIST'S ARCHIVE

DISCWORLD

NUNC ID VIDES NUNC NE VIDES

GRUNE | OCTEDAY

UNSEEN UNIVERSITY

DIARY

TERRY PRATCHETT
STEPHEN BRIGGS
PAUL KIDBY

ACVTVS ID
VERBERAT

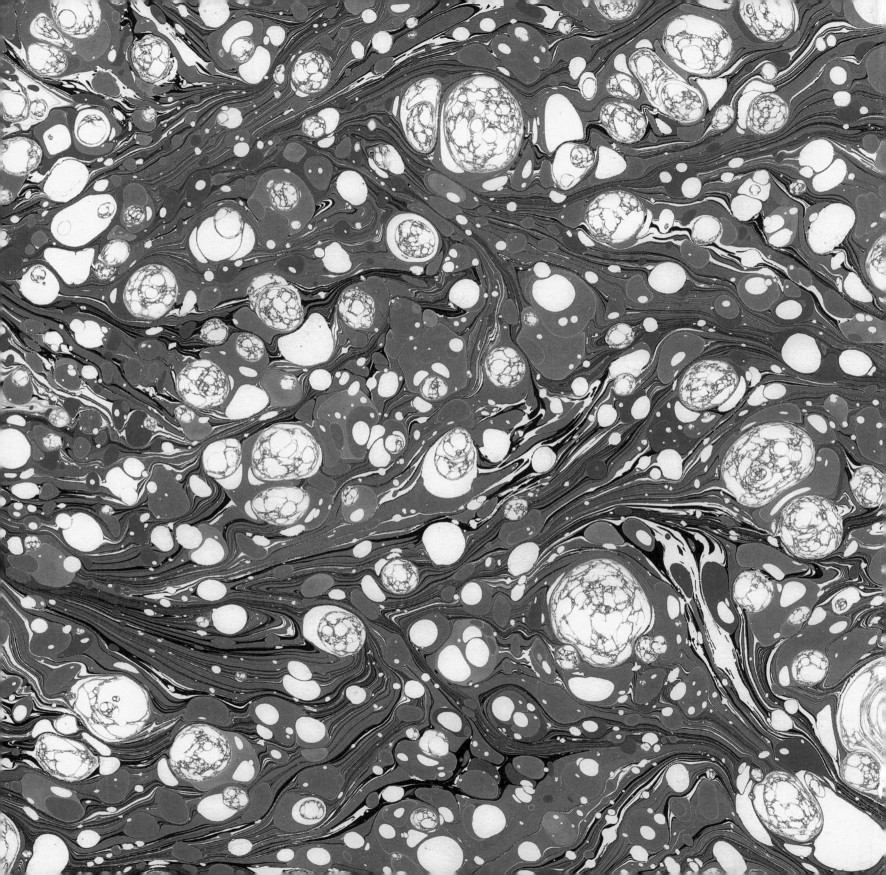